Thomas Thomason Perowne

Obadiah and Jonah

with notes and introduction

Thomas Thomason Perowne

Obadiah and Jonah
with notes and introduction

ISBN/EAN: 9783337400798

Printed in Europe, USA, Canada, Australia, Japan

Cover: Foto ©Andreas Hilbeck / pixelio.de

More available books at **www.hansebooks.com**

The Cambridge Bible for Schools and Colleges.

GENERAL EDITOR:—J. J. S. PEROWNE, D.D.,
DEAN OF PETERBOROUGH.

OBADIAH AND JONAH,

WITH NOTES AND INTRODUCTION

BY

THE VEN. T. T. PEROWNE, B.D.

ARCHDEACON OF NORWICH;
LATE FELLOW OF CORPUS CHRISTI COLLEGE, CAMBRIDGE.

EDITED FOR THE SYNDICS OF THE UNIVERSITY PRESS.

Cambridge:
AT THE UNIVERSITY PRESS.
1889

PREFACE

BY THE GENERAL EDITOR.

THE General Editor of *The Cambridge Bible for Schools* thinks it right to say that he does not hold himself responsible either for the interpretation of particular passages which the Editors of the several Books have adopted, or for any opinion on points of doctrine that they may have expressed. In the New Testament more especially questions arise of the deepest theological import, on which the ablest and most conscientious interpreters have differed and always will differ. His aim has been in all such cases to leave each Contributor to the unfettered exercise of his own judgment, only taking care that mere controversy should as far as possible be avoided. He has contented himself chiefly with a careful revision of the notes, with pointing out omissions, with suggesting occasionally a reconsideration of some question, or a fuller treatment of difficult passages, and the like.

Beyond this he has not attempted to interfere, feeling it better that each Commentary should have its own individual character, and being convinced that freshness and variety of treatment are more than a compensation for any lack of uniformity in the Series.

DEANERY, PETERBOROUGH.

CONTENTS.

*** The Text adopted in this Edition is that of Dr Scrivener's *Cambridge Paragraph Bible*. A few variations from the ordinary Text, chiefly in the spelling of certain words, and in the use of italics, will be noticed. For the principles adopted by Dr Scrivener as regards the printing of the Text see his Introduction to the *Paragraph Bible*, published by the Cambridge University Press.

INTRODUCTION.

I. THE AUTHOR.

OF the personal history of Obadiah nothing is known. The name which he bears, "servant of Yah," or "worshipper of Yah," is a common one in the Old Testament. We are specially familiar with it as borne by the godly chamberlain of Ahab in the time of Elijah (1 Kings xviii. 3—16). But neither with him, nor with any other of the persons who are called by it in the sacred history, can the author of this Book be identified.

II. THE DATE.

Considerable difference of opinion exists with reference to the time when Obadiah lived and prophesied. The dates assigned to him by different critics range over a period of several centuries. The principal considerations, on which the decision of the question depends, are

1. The place which he occupies among the Minor Prophets ;

2. The capture of Jerusalem to which he refers in vv. 11—14; and

3. The subject-matter which he has in common with other Old Testament writers.

1. With respect to the first of these considerations, it is true that the order in which the Minor Prophets are placed in the arrangement of the Canon is, as a general rule, so far chronological, that the place which is occupied by a prophet should be

taken into the account in assigning to him his date. The twelve are broken into two chief groups. The eight (omitting Obadiah) which stand first belong to the period before the captivity in Babylon. The three which stand last came after that event. If, therefore, Obadiah lived and prophesied at the time of the capture of Jerusalem by the Chaldeans, we should expect to find him placed, not where we do, between Amos who prophesied in the reigns of Uzziah in Judah and Jeroboam II. in Israel (Amos i. 1), and Jonah who was probably of about the same date (2 Kings xiv. 25, comp. Introd. to Jonah, c. I.), but between the two groups of prophets who flourished respectively before and after the captivity, i. e. immediately before Haggai. It has been suggested, however, that the weight of this consideration is counterbalanced by the fact, that the prophecy of Obadiah is in effect an expansion of the short prediction against Edom, which occurs at the close of the prophecy of Amos (ix. 12). This fact may account for the departure from chronological order in the case of Obadiah by the framers of the Canon, and may be a sufficient reason for his being placed among those earlier prophets, who were not really his contemporaries.

2: The second principal consideration connected with the date of this Book is the reference which it contains to the capture of Jerusalem. We know from Old Testament history of four occasions on which that city was taken. Can we then identify the capture here referred to with any one of them? And if so, how far does it help us to decide the time at which Obadiah lived?

(a) Jerusalem was taken by Shishak king of Egypt in the reign of Rehoboam (1 Kings xiv. 25, 26; 2 Chron. xii. 1—12). But we read in the Book of Chronicles that the king and his nobles humbled themselves under the rebuke of Shemaiah the prophet, and that consequently Shishak, though he carried away the treasures both of the Temple and of the palace, did not inflict such evils either on the city or on its inhabitants as Obadiah describes. This therefore cannot be the incident referred to.

(*b*) For similar reasons Obadiah's description cannot be held to refer to the sacking of Jerusalem by the Philistines and Arabians in the reign of Jehoram (2 Chron. xxi. 16, 17). The blow on that occasion seems to have fallen almost exclusively on the king's house.

(*c*) The defeat of Amaziah by Jehoash was followed indeed by the breaking down of the wall of Jerusalem (2 Kings xiv. 8—14; 2 Chron. xxv. 17—24), but the language of Obadiah is descriptive of some more terrible calamity and "destruction" than that, and the invasion of Judah by an Israelitish army could not be spoken of, as it is by the prophet, as "the day that the strangers carried away captive his forces, and foreigners entered into his gates" (ver. 11).

(*d*) There only remains therefore to be identified, as the event to which allusion is made by Obadiah, and as adequately satisfying the terms of his description, the capture and destruction of Jerusalem by the Chaldeans. We do not find indeed in the historical record of that event any mention of the part taken by the Edomites with the Chaldeans against the Jews ; but this fact, for the knowledge of which we are indebted to the graphic utterances of Obadiah, is quite in keeping with the probabilities of the case, and with the ancient and bitter hostility of Edom towards Israel. So early as the time of the Exodus they had churlishly refused them a passage through their country (Num. xx. 14—21), and though conquered by David (2 Sam. viii. 14; comp. 1 Kings ix. 26), and again with circumstances of great cruelty by Amaziah (2 Chron. xxv. 11, 12), they avenged themselves in later years during the decline of the Jewish kingdom, by recovering their lost cities and making incursions into southern Palestine (2 Kings xvi. 6; where "Edomites" (R.V.) and not "Syrians" (A.V.) is now generally received as the true reading; 2 Chron. xxviii. 17). It is only natural therefore to suppose, that when Nebu-chadnezzar advanced against Jerusalem the Edomites gladly welcomed the opportunity of revenge, and joining his forces exultingly bore their part in the degradation and ruin of their ancient foe.

When, however, we have thus succeeded in fixing the historical event which Obadiah has in view, it is important clearly to understand how far it helps us to determine the time at which he wrote.

There can be no doubt that as is now generally admitted the rendering of the A. V. in vv. 11—14, "Thou shouldest not have," "Neither shouldest thou have," etc. is grammatically incorrect. What the prophet really says is—

"In the day of thy standing on the other side, in the day of strangers carrying away captive his forces, when foreigners entered into his gates and cast lots upon Jerusalem, thou too (wast) as one of them. But look not on the day of thy brother in the day of his becoming a stranger, and rejoice not at the children of Judah in the day of their destruction, and enlarge not thy mouth in the day of trouble. Enter not into the gate of my people in the day of their destruction. Look not, thou too, on their calamity in the day of their destruction, and stretch not forth (thy hand) on their substance in the day of their destruction. And stand not at the cross-way to cut off his fugitives, and deliver not up his survivors in the day of trouble."

Now here the prophet clearly regards the calamity to which he refers as having already come upon Jerusalem, and he sees the Edomites already engaged as abettors in that calamity, and earnestly dissuades them from the course which they are pursuing. It is obvious that he might well have used this language, and that all the conditions required by the passage would have been satisfactorily fulfilled, if he had written immediately after the sacking of Jerusalem by the Chaldeans, and when, as may not improbably have been the case, the Edomites and other neighbouring tribes were still harassing the Jews, even after Nebuchadnezzar's army had been withdrawn. In this case the prophet would be simply describing what had just gone on, or was then actually going on, under his own eyes. He would be the historian of the past as regards Edom's sin ; the fore-teller of the future only as regards his punishment.

But when the nature of prophecy is taken into account we are met by the consideration, that in the language before us

Obadiah may be describing not that which was already past or present when he lived and wrote, but only that which was past or present as regards the point of time into which in prophetic vision he was rapt. In other words that he was borne by the spirit of prophecy into the future, and looked thence upon the sin of Edom as already done or doing, although in point of fact it had not yet been perpetrated.

No safe conclusion therefore as to Obadiah's date can be drawn from his language in this place. The drama enacted before his eyes may equally well, so far as his description of it is concerned, recall the past, or anticipate the future. In itself considered it determines nothing as to the date of the prophecy.

We must then fall back upon other considerations. And here the probability would certainly seem to be, that Obadiah is commissioned to foretell the punishment of Edom for the recent wrongdoing which he so vividly depicts. His prophecy would thus have been delivered shortly after the destruction of the city, or between its first capture and final destruction, by the Chaldeans. The argument that that event could not have happened when the prophet wrote, because God does not warn men against sins already committed, rests on the assumption that it is a *warning*, which the prophet is here directed to convey. But it may equally well have been a denunciation of sin already committed, on account of which the threatened judgment was about to fall. And that it is so is rendered probable by the consideration, that the prophecy was not apparently designed for the warning of the Edomites, whom so far as we know it never reached, but for the comfort and encouragement of the faithful amongst the Jews, to whom it gave assurance not only of the approaching overthrow of Edom and restoration of Israel, but of that far brighter and more glorious future, of which those nearer fulfilments of the prophecy were the type and the pledge.

3. The probability as to the date of Obadiah, which has been thus arrived at, gains strength when we lay the contents of his prophecy beside those of other Old Testament Books, in

which a similarity of language or of subject may be traced, and of which the date has been satisfactorily ascertained.

(*a*) Such a similarity of thought and diction has been supposed to exist between the prophets Obadiah and Joel. Some persons have even gone so far as to affirm that the words "as the Lord hath said" (Joel ii. 32 [Heb. iii. 5]), point to a prophetic word already known, viz.: to Obad. 17 (Keil), and that therefore Obadiah must have been the contemporary or precursor of Joel. But the phrase, "as the Lord hath said," may be merely that claim on the part of Joel of divine origin and authority for his own utterances, which is so commonly made by other prophets ; and the expressions used by the two writers though similar are by no means identical. The whole verse in Joel is—

"And it shall come to pass, that whosoever shall call on the name of the Lord shall be delivered : for in mount Zion and in Jerusalem shall be deliverance, as the Lord hath said, and in the remnant whom the Lord shall call;"

and in Obadiah

"But upon mount Zion shall be deliverance, and there shall be holiness; and the house of Jacob shall possess their possessions."

The resemblance between these two verses is far too slight to justify the assumption that one is a quotation from the other, and the rather because the subject to which they refer is different in the two prophets. The same may be said of the other expressions which Joel and Obadiah have in common. They are not of a character to warrant the conclusion, that one of these writers borrowed them from the other. Even if they were, it would obviously remain to be decided to which of them they originally belonged. But indeed the theory of quotation may easily be pressed too far in the case of the Old Testament writers. We need not always suppose that "a man has bored a hole in another man's tank," because his thoughts flow in the same channel, or clothe themselves in the same language.

(*b*) The relation of Obadiah to Jeremiah is of a very different kind. It is impossible to lay side by side the denunciation of Edom by Obadiah (vv. 1—9) and the prophecy of Jeremiah on the same subject (xlix. 7—22) without being convinced that they are either derived from a common source or that one of them is a reproduction of the other.

The theory of a common source is naturally adopted by that school of critics, whose *rôle* it is to reduce the writings of the Old Testament to a kind of literary patch-work; requiring us to believe on the evidence of supposed differences of style and language, which their critical faculty can detect, that the component elements of a Book, a verse here and a paragraph there, are to be attributed to different dates and authors. To such free handling this short prophecy has been subjected. The first section of it (vv. 1—7), we are told, "looks as if it had been taken from a larger work of our prophet's, in which he had given a collection of Oracles concerning foreign nations. He knew quite well from the sources of his collection that the piece concerning Edom, which he wished to place as the superstructure above his own, was by a prophet Obadiah; and we have no reason to doubt the historical accuracy of his knowledge[1]." (Ewald). The second section (vv. 8—15), according to this critic, is composed of three verses (8—10) from the old prophet,

---

[1] This older prophet, we are told, the true Obadiah, whose name has been left standing by the later compiler of our present Book of Obadiah, lived and prophesied at the time of the inroads of Rezin and Pekah, which have been referred to above (2 Kings xvi. 6; 2 Chron. xxviii. 17). "Cheated of their hopes in this direction (Jerusalem), they seem to have directed their whole strength, as a preliminary measure, to the conquest of the ample territories beyond the Jordan, extending to the bay of Elath, which had been retained ever since their acquisition under Uzziah; and in this quarter their undertaking was completely successful. King Rezin, who appears throughout as far more powerful than Pekah, conquered the whole of these possessions of Judah as far as Elath on the Red Sea, banished all the Jews, even those who had doubtless been settled there for a long time for purposes of commerce, from this important commercial city, and restored it again to the Idumeans, who from that time established themselves there still more firmly than before. The Idumeans themselves, when freed from the dominion of Judah, refortified in the strongest manner their rocky capital (Sela, Petra), and were once more in a position to indulge to the fullest extent their ancient propensity of falling upon the cities of Judah in marauding expeditions...... These events afforded occasion to Obadiah, a contemporary prophet of Jerusalem, to direct the word of God against the pride of the Idumeans, which had suddenly swollen to such a height." Ewald, *History of Israel*, IV. 159 (Carpenter's Translation).

followed by four of the compiler's own (11—14), and then by another from the ancient source. The third section is in like manner composite, v. 16 being written by the compiler, vv. 17, 18, borrowed as before, and vv. 19—21 written by himself again. But this kind of criticism, always arbitrary and precarious, seems nowhere more out of place than in the brief prophecy of Obadiah. As a literary composition this short piece is a complete and united whole. The train of thought is quite unbroken. The style is uniform. The parts cohere perfectly. On this account it seems difficult to believe, that Obadiah had before him the substance of any earlier prophecy which he incorporated into his own, or that he culled and fitted together scattered sentences from Jeremiah.

The most probable conclusion is, that Obadiah, stirred by the recent wrongs inflicted by the Edomites upon his people, wrongs which perhaps he had himself witnessed, was commissioned to pour forth this brief denunciation against them ; while Jeremiah, his contemporary, took up and repeated shortly after in his own more elaborate parable of reproach much of what his brother prophet had uttered. This view accords with the fact that the matter common to the two is contained in a short consecutive passage of eight verses in Obadiah, while it is scattered over a paragraph of sixteen verses in Jeremiah and is set in additional matter of his own. It accords also with the use which Jeremiah elsewhere makes of earlier prophecies than his own (comp. Jer. xlviii. 29, 30, with Is. xvi. 6, and Jer. xlix. 27 with Amos i. 4). On the whole, it seems not unlikely that Obadiah prophesied in or about the year in which Jerusalem was taken by Nebuchadnezzar, B.C. 588 or 587, and that Jeremiah, whose Book is not arranged in chronological order, and to whose prophecy against Edom no certain date can on internal evidence be assigned, delivered that prophecy shortly afterwards.

It is a confirmation of this view that the Book of Lamentations written by Jeremiah at the time when the horrors attendant upon the capture of Jerusalem were being enacted before his eyes, contains a prophecy of the coming destruction of Edom and recovery of the daughter of Zion, which is in substance identical with the prophecy of Obadiah. "Rejoice, and be glad," the prophet cries in bitter irony, "O daughter of Edom, that dwellest in the land of Uz." Exult maliciously as thou dost in the calamity of Jerusalem; but know that thy malicious triumph is but for a moment. "The cup also shall pass through unto thee: thou shalt be drunken, and shalt make thyself naked." But for the daughter of Zion a happy future of restoration from captivity and of Messianic hope beyond is in store. Her pardon is complete, and stands out in bright contrast with the punishment with which the prophet again threatens Edom. "The punishment of thine iniquity is accomplished, O daughter of Zion; he will no more carry thee away into captivity: he will visit thine iniquity, O daughter of Edom; he will discover thy sins" (Lam. iv. 21, 22).

(c) Two other Old Testament denunciations against Edom belong to the same period of Jewish history, and serve to throw light upon the prophecy of Obadiah. The prophet Ezekiel exercising his office during the captivity in Babylon, at the commencement of which we have seen reason to place the cruel conduct of the Edomites and Obadiah's condemnation of it, delivers two predictions of woe against them. In the first and shorter of these it is for the same reason that Obadiah alleges, viz., "because that Edom hath dealt against the house of Judah by taking vengeance, and hath greatly offended and revenged himself upon them," that destruction is to come upon him. And in this also the two prophets are agreed, viz. that Israel is the destined minister of God's wrath against Edom. "I will lay my vengeance upon Edom by the hand of my people Israel" (Ezekiel xxv. 12—14; comp. Obad. 18). In the longer and later prophecy the same cause is given, the continuous character of the hatred which culminated in the destruction of Jerusalem being pointed out, for the coming doom of Edom. "Thou hast had a perpetual hatred, and hast shed the blood of the children of Israel by the force of the sword in the time of their calamity, in the time that their iniquity had an end" (Ezekiel xxxv. 5; comp. v. 15). Here however the prophecy of Edom's impending doom (xxxv.

1—15) is followed, as in Obadiah, by the joyful announcement of Israel's approaching prosperity (xxxvi. 1—15).

(*d*) There remains a yet later reference to the crowning injury inflicted by Edom upon Israel, which it is interesting to notice in this connection. It occurs in the cxxxviith Psalm. "In all probability the writer was a Levite, who had been carried away by the armies of Nebuchadnezzar when Jerusalem was sacked and the Temple destroyed, and who was one of the first, as soon as the edict of Cyrus was published, to return to Jerusalem. He is again in his own land. He sees again the old familiar scenes. The mountains and the valleys that his foot trod in youth are before him. The great landmarks are the same, and yet the change is terrible. The spoiler has been in his home, his vines and his fig trees have been cut down, the House of his God is a heap of ruins. His heart is heavy with a sense of desolation, and bitter with the memory of wrong and insult from which he has but lately escaped.

" He takes his harp, the companion of his exile, the cherished relic of happier days,—the harp which he could not string at the bidding of his conquerors by the waters of Babylon ; and now with faltering hand he sweeps the strings, first in low, plaintive, melancholy cadence pouring out his griefs, and then with a loud crash of wild and stormy numbers of his verse, he raises the pæan of vengeance over his foes....As he broods over his wrongs, as he looks upon the desolation of his country, as he remembers with peculiar bitterness how they who ought to have been allies took part with the enemies of Jerusalem in the fatal day of her overthrow, there bursts forth the terrible cry for vengeance ; vengeance first on the false kindred, and next on the proud conquerors of his race.

" Deepest of all was the indignation roused by the sight of the nearest of kin, the race of Esau, often allied to Judah, often independent, now bound by the closest union with the power that was truly the common enemy of both. There was an intoxication of delight in the wild Edomite chiefs, as at each successive stroke against the venerable walls they shouted, 'Down with it! down with it! even to the ground.' They stood in the

passes to intercept the escape of those who would have fled
down to the Jordan valley; they betrayed the fugitives; they
indulged their barbarous revels on the Temple hill. Long and
loud has been the wail of execration which has gone up from the
Jewish nation against Edom. It is the one imprecation which
breaks forth from the Lamentations of Jeremiah: it is the cul-
mination of the fierce threats of Ezekiel: it is the sole purpose
of the short, sharp cry of Obadiah; it is the bitterest drop in
the sad recollections of the Israelite captives by the waters of
Babylon: and the one warlike strain of the Evangelical Prophet
is inspired by the hope that the Divine Conqueror should come
knee-deep in Idumæan blood (Lam. iv. 21, 22; Ezek. xxv. 8,
12—14; Obad. 1—21; Jer. xlix. 7—22; Is. lxiii. 1—4)." Perowne
on *the Psalms*, and Stanley, *Jewish Church*, II. p. 556, as quoted
there.

III. THE CONTENTS.

1. The prophecy flows on in one continuous and unbroken
whole; but it may for convenience be divided into two principal
parts or sections:

   i.   The destruction of Edom (vv. 1—16).
   ii. The restoration of Israel (vv. 17—21).

The first of these sections has again three paragraphs, or sub-
sections, of which the first (vv. 1—9) announces the punishment
of Edom; the second (vv. 10—14) is a quasi-parenthesis, giving
the reason why the punishment has come upon her; and the
third (vv. 15, 16) resumes the denunciation against Edom and
extends it to the heathen generally.

The following is a brief analysis of the whole:—

The prophet is charged with heavy tidings from Jehovah
against Edom. The heathen nations are summoned against her
to battle and shall bring her low (vv. 1, 2). Confident in the
strength of her natural position, safe as she deems herself in the
inaccessible rock-hewn chambers and impregnable fastnesses of
Petra, she fears no evil. Yet even thence the hand of the Lord

will bring her down (vv. 3, 4). It is no ordinary predatory incur-
sion of robber hordes, who take their fill of plunder and depart,
that shall overtake her (v. 5). She shall be utterly stripped (v. 6).
Her confederates and allies shall treacherously desert and take
part against her (v. 7). The famed wisdom of her sages shall
fail, and the courage of her valiant men forsake them. Without
counsel to guide, or strength to defend her, she shall be brought
to complete destruction (vv. 8, 9). The cause of the punishment that shall thus come upon her is the violent and malicious
conduct, which, regardless of the ties of kindred and the claims
of a common ancestry, she displayed against the children or
Israel in the time of their calamity (vv. 10—14). For this, in
the approaching day of God's visitation upon the heathen at
large, Edom shall specially come into remembrance before Him,
and with the measure with which she has meted it shall be
measured to her again (vv. 15, 16). But to the house of Jacob
shall deliverance and restoration be vouchsafed (v. 17). They
shall be the instruments in God's hand of completing the punishment of Edom, which the heathen had begun (v. 18). They
shall dispossess the invaders of their country, and shall spread
in all directions throughout their own land (vv. 19, 20). And
this destruction of Edom and restoration of Israel shall eventu-
ally issue in the promised, though still future and long-looked-
for consummation, when "the kingdom shall be the Lord's"
(v. 21).

2. It is evident from this analysis that the Edomites were
still in possession of their own land when Obadiah wrote. The
natural conformation of that land was, as the prophet intimates,
such as might well foster a proud sense of security in a warlike
and independent race. The territory of Edom proper comprised
a narrow strip, about a hundred miles long by twenty broad,
reaching along the eastern side of the Arabah, and extending
from nearly the southern extremity of the Dead Sea to Elath at
the head of the Arabian gulf. It was throughout a mountainous
district, though as is not uncommonly the case in such locali-
ties, the clefts and terraces of its rocks and hills abounded in
rich and fertile soil. Hence its common Biblical name, "the

Mount of Esau" (Obad. 8, 9, 19, 21) and "Mount Seir" (Gen.
xiv. 6; Deut. ii. 1, 5). The ancient capital of Edom appears to
have been Bozrah (Gen. xxxvi. 33; Is. xxxiv. 6; Jer. xlix. 13).
But when Obadiah wrote Selah or Petra had taken its place.
The well-known features of this remarkable city, as regards both
the famous defile which was then the chief way of access to it,
and the nature of its dwellings, hewn out of the solid rock, were
calculated, as Obadiah again reminds us, to raise to the utmost
pitch the spirit of haughty defiance, with which the Edomites
contemplated the prospect of attack. But the prophet warns
them that their confidence is vain. They had made the invasion
of Judea by the armies of Nebuchadnezzar an occasion for the
cruel and malicious indulgence of their ancient hatred of the
Jews. They had aided and abetted in the humiliation of those
whom they ought rather to have helped and befriended. For
this the prophet announces a two-fold chastisement in store for
them.

3. The first blow is to be struck by "the heathen," to whom
the herald of Jehovah is sent to gather them together against
Edom, and who are to be the agents and witnesses of her
humiliation (Obad. 1, 2, 7). Of the fulfilment of this first prophecy against Edom we have clear historical proof, though we
do not possess any definite record of the exact time and circumstances of its accomplishment. We know certainly that at least
three centuries before the Christian era Petra was in the
possession, not of the Edomites, but of the Nabathæans, a
powerful race, who whether descended from Nebaioth the son
of Ishmael (Gen. xxv. 13) or not, were in all probability of
Aramaic or Syro-Chaldean origin. (Smith's *Bible Dict.* Artt.
Edom, Nebaioth.) For Diodorus Siculus relates that Antigonus,
one of the generals of Alexander the Great, who at his death
succeeded to a part of his dominions, "undertook an expedition
against the country of the Arabians who are called Nabathæans[1]," and in the absence of its defenders, by his general

---

[1] " ἐπεβάλετο στρατεύειν ἐπὶ τὴν χώραν τῶν Ἀράβων, τῶν καλουμένων
Ναβαταίων." Diod. Sic. lib. 19. 730—733, where further particulars of
a second expedition under Demetrius are given.

Athenæus seized and spoiled Petra. Of the history of the Edomites, from the time of their misconduct at the capture of Jerusalem (B.C. 588), up to the time of this invasion of their former territory by Antigonus (B.C. 312), we do not know enough to enable us certainly to fix the date of their dispossession by the Nabathæans. We learn, however, from Josephus that, in fulfilment of the prophecy of Jeremiah (xliii. 8—13), "in the fifth year after the destruction of Jerusalem, which was the 23rd of the reign of Nebuchadnezzar, he made an expedition against Cœle-Syria; and when he had possessed himself of it, he made war against the Ammonites and Moabites, and when he had brought all these nations under subjection, he fell upon Egypt in order to overthrow it[1]." It can hardly be doubted that Edom proper was included in the country thus conquered by Nebu-chadnezzar. It would have been a strange oversight to leave that stronghold behind him unsubdued, when he moved forward towards Egypt; and it is observable that in the prophecy of Jeremiah which predicts this very subjection of Ammon and Moab to Nebuchadnezzar, "the king of Edom" is the first potentate summoned to yield (Jer. xxvii. 3); while it is added "now have I given all these lands into the hand of Nebuchad-nezzar, king of Babylon" (v. 6). It is therefore, to say the least, a highly probable supposition, that Nebuchadnezzar having at this time possessed himself of Edom, transplanted thither a Chaldean colony of Nabathæans, to take the place of the Edomites, whom he had defeated and expelled[2]. But whether this highly probable supposition be accepted or not, the historical fact of the occupation of Petra by the Naba-thæans remains, and carries with it the fulfilment of Obadiah's

---

[1] *Antiq.* l. x. c. 9. § 7 (Whiston).

[2] With reference to this Ewald writes: "Accordingly, five years after the destruction of the capital, a new struggle arose, which ter-minated in the exile of seven hundred and forty-five persons...... (Jer. lii. 30). At the same time, war had at length openly broken out between the Chaldeans and the Moabites and Ammonites, into which these Judahites certainly allowed themselves to be drawn; and Ishmael then perhaps received the reward he had earned." Ewald, *Hist. of Isr.* vol. IV. p. 276 (Carpenter's Trans.).

prediction concerning Edom, that the heathen should "rise up against her in battle", and dispossess her of her strongholds, and "bring her down to the ground".

4. The second and more complete overthrow of the Edomites was to be effected by the Jews (vv. 18, 19), "delivered" and restored to their own "possessions" (v. 17). The steps in the fulfilment of this prophecy can be very clearly traced. The Edomites, expelled as we have seen from their own country, spread westward, and during the Babylonish captivity and the subsequent depression of the Jews, possessed themselves of the territory of the Amalekites, and of many towns in Southern Palestine, including Hebron. When however the military prowess of the Jews revived in the time of the Maccabees, Judas Maccabæus attacked and defeated the Edomites (B.C. 166), and recovered the cities of Southern Palestine which they had taken[1]. Subsequently (B.C. 135), John Hyrcanus completed the conquest of the Edomites, and compelled them to submit to circumcision and to be merged in the Jewish nation[2]. At a still later period, in the troublous times of the Zealots and of the Roman war (A.D. 66), Simon of Gerasa having gained access to Idumea through the treachery of one of the Edomite generals, "did not only ravage the cities and villages, but lay waste the whole country." "And", in the graphic words of Josephus, "as one may see all the woods behind despoiled of their leaves by locusts, after they have been there, so was there nothing left behind Simon's army, but a desert. Some places they burnt down; some they utterly demolished, and whatsoever grew in the country they either trod

---

[1] "But Judas and his brethren did not leave off fighting with the Idumeans; but pressed upon them on all sides, and took from them the city of Hebron, and demolished all its fortifications, and set its towers on fire," &c. Joseph. *Ant.* XII. 8, § 6. Comp. 1 Macc. v. 3, 65.

[2] "Hyrcanus took also Dora and Marissa, cities of Idumea, and subdued all the Idumeans, and permitted them to stay in the country, if they would circumcise themselves, and make use of the laws of the Jews. And they were so desirous of living in the country of their forefathers, that they submitted to the use of circumcision, and of the rest of the Jewish ways of living. At which time, therefore, this befell them, that they were hereafter no other than Jews" (Ib. XIII. 9, § 1; where see Whiston's note).

it down, or fed upon it; and by their marches they made the
ground that was cultivated harder and more tractable than that
which was barren. In short there was no sign remaining of those
places that had been laid waste, that ever they had a being[1]".

5. But beyond the overthrow of Edom and restoration of
Israel, which were literally fulfilled, the prophecy has undoubtedly a wider range, and a more distant scope.

A typical or allegorical meaning has very generally been assigned to Edom in this and other Old Testament prophecies.
When their ancient foe had passed away, the Jews, not un-
naturally perhaps, recognised Rome, their latest oppressor, in
the Edom of their prophets, and comforted themselves with the
belief that on this second Edom, as on the first, the predicted
vengeance would one day fall. Thus we find their Rabbis
asserting that "Janus, the first king of Latium, was grandson
of Esau," and that both Julius Cæsar and Titus were Edomites.
When the Roman Empire became Christian, then Christians
generally came to be regarded as Edomites by the Jews. The
persecutions which Christians have heaped upon them go far, it
must be confessed, to justify the reference, and it is scarcely
surprising that with modern Jews it is a canon of interpretation that by the Edomites are meant the Christians. Their
Messiah when he comes is to gather Israel from all the countries of their dispersion into their own land, and destroy their
Edomite, that is Christian, oppressors. (Specimens of this kind
of interpretation of the prophecies of Obadiah may be found in
the *Dictionary of the Bible*, Art. *Obadiah*.) With the Christian Church Edom has been held to represent the enemies of
herself and of her Lord, while the restoration of Israel to their
own land and their diffusion throughout its limits have been interpreted to signify the spread of Christianity throughout the
world. That such an allegorical (Gal. iv. 24), or as it is sometimes called spiritual interpretation of Old Testament prophecy,
is rightly recognised by the Christian Church we cannot doubt.
She has succeeded for the time to the inheritance of Israel of
old. Her children are the seed of Abraham (Gal. iii. 29). All

---

[1] *Bell. Jud*. IV. c. 9, § 7.

the promises are theirs (2 Cor. i. 20). To her and to them all
the glowing future belongs. They shall share His throne and
His dominion when "the kingdom shall be the Lord's."

But the question still remains, whether beyond not only those
first literal fulfilments of this and similar Old Testament prophecies, which may be traced in the past or present history of the
world, but beyond also that spiritual or allegorical fulfilment of
them which the Church of Christ is warranted in claiming and
enjoying for herself, there may not lie yet another fulfilment
of many of them which, combining both the literal and spiritual features of those earlier fulfilments, and comprehending in
its wide embrace the Jew as well as the Gentile, may fully
satisfy the conditions and exhaust the terms of those ancient
predictions. That such a fulfilment was contemplated, and is
to be expected still, it seems reasonable to believe. The canon
of interpretation which excludes the Jew, as such, from any
participation in the promised future, breaks down continually
when we apply it to the prophetical writings of the Old
Testament. The literal and the spiritual elements refuse to
yield to its requirements. We cannot, without doing violence
to language and connection, dissociate the blessing and the
curse, heaping all the one upon the Ebal of the Jewish nation, while we crown with all the other the Gerizim of the
Church of Christ. Even if these literary difficulties, grammatical, contextual, critical, could be overcome, the New Testament would step in to forbid the process. There too the
future of the Jew, as such, is painted in glowing colours (Rom.
xi.). And the history of the Jews throughout the long centuries
of their dispersion and oppression, their inextinguishable vitality,
their indomitable energy, their remarkable ability and success,
their presence as an alien and foreign element, distinct and refusing to merge or to disappear, in every nation of the earth,
points in the same direction. It is a standing prophecy not only
of their destined conversion as a nation to the faith of Christ,
but of their future restoration to their own land. "And so all
Israel shall be saved : as it is written, There shall come out of
Sion the Deliverer, and shall turn away ungodliness from Jacob"
(Rom. xi. 26). And then "the kingdom shall be the Lord's."

OBADIAH.

1—16. The Destruction of Edom. 1—9. The Punishment of Edom foretold.

1

T HE vision of Obadiah.
Thus saith the Lord GOD concerning Edom ;

1—16. THE DESTRUCTION OF EDOM. 1—9. THE PUNISHMENT OF EDOM FORETOLD.

1. *The vision of Obadiah.*] This is the short Title of this short Book. It tells us the name of the Author, which is all that we know of him, and the nature of his work.

The vision] This word, like its cognate verb, when it is used with reference to prophetic revelation (e.g. Hab. i. 1; Isaiah i. 1; ii. 1; Nah. i. 1, comp. "seer," 1 Chron. xxi. 9 and the explanation given in 1 Sam. ix. 9, where however the Heb. word for "seer" is not the same) properly signifies that which appears as it were before the eyes of the prophet, the picture which is represented to his mind in prophetic ecstasy. In that strict sense, part at least of what here follows was the vision of Obadiah. He sees the Edomites in the rocky fastnesses of Petra, like the eagles on their crags (*vv.* 3, 4). He beholds them taking part against the Israelites in the day of their calamity, and as a spectator of their actions cries out to them repeatedly, "Do it not" (*vv.* 11—14). But the word comes to be used in a wider sense, and is often, as here, the title of a whole Book, in which, together with visions proper, historical and other matter is contained (comp. Isaiah i. 1 with 2 Chron. xxxii. 32).

Obadiah] i.e. servant, or worshipper of Jehovah.

Thus saith the Lord God concerning Edom] This is not a second title of the Book. It does not stand as an independent sentence, but is closely connected with what follows. The word "her" at the end of the verse and the direct addresses without mention of name, *vv.* 2—5, refer to and require the word "Edom" in this clause. It is rather the opening announcement of the prophet, that all that he is about to utter is not his own word, but Jehovah's. The remainder of the verse follows logically, rather than formally, upon this announcement. In verse 2, Jehovah is introduced as the speaker.

We have heard a rumour from the LORD,
And an ambassador is sent among the heathen,
Arise ye, and let us rise up against her in battle.

2   Behold, I have made thee small among the heathen :
Thou *art* greatly despised.

We have heard] This has been taken to mean, "I, and other prophets of my own or earlier times," or "I, and my countrymen," implying, in this latter case, "that the tidings were of the greatest interest to Israel, and would afford it consolation." (Delitzsch.) But the absence of the personal pronoun in the Hebrew, and the use of the singular number, "I have heard," by Jeremiah in the parallel passage (xlix. 14) seem rather to shew that "We" has here no special emphasis. To the prophet as a Jew the world was divided into two parts, his own countrymen and the heathen. "A rumour," he says, "has reached us : a herald is sent to them."

rumour] lit. **hearing**. The same Hebrew word is rendered "report" Is. liii. 1, and elsewhere. (Comp. ἀκοαὶ πολέμων, Matt. xxiv. 6.) It means here tidings (R.V.), or message. There is no idea of uncertainty as in the English word rumour.

ambassador] or **a messenger** (comp. Prov. xiii. 17; xxv. 13). The meaning of the word seems to be, to go on circuit; or as we should say to go round, from nation to nation. Jeremiah describes Nebuchadnezzar, king of Babylon, as fighting against Jerusalem and against all the cities thereof with "all his army and all the kingdoms of the earth of his dominion, and all the people" (xxxiv. 1). His army would doubtless be of the same composite character when he subsequently turned his hand against Edom.

Arise ye, and let us rise up] This may either be taken as being throughout the address of the messenger or herald to the nations whom he visits, inciting them to arise, and associating himself with them in the invitation which he gives ; or it may be the call of the herald and the response of the nations, heard as it were and recorded by the prophet— "Arise," says he; "Let us arise," say they.   Or yet again, the words may be throughout those of the heathen exhorting one another to obey the summons of the herald, whose address to them is not recorded but left to be gathered by the reader from the effect which it produces. This last is most forcible and most in accordance with the graphic style of Obadiah.   He hears the call to arms passing to and fro, brief and eager, "Arise ye," "Let us arise," as Jehovah's herald pursues his onward course.   The parallel passage in Jeremiah, however, if it is to be regarded as a version of them in prose, favours the first of these interpretations of the words.

2.   *I have made thee...thou art*] Jehovah is now the speaker. "I have made thee small" in my purpose, which though its accomplishment is still future is as certain as though it were already executed. "Thou art," already in inevitable destiny, "greatly despised." There is nothing to commend the view of Calvin and others that ver. 2 is intro-

The pride of thine heart hath deceived thee,   3
Thou that dwellest in the clefts of the rock, whose habi-
    tation *is* high ;
That saith in his heart, Who shall bring me down *to* the
    ground ?
Though thou exalt *thyself* as the eagle,   4
And though *thou* set thy nest among the stars,
Thence will I bring thee down, saith the LORD.
If thieves came to thee, if robbers by night, (how art thou 5
    cut off !)
Would they not have stolen till they had enough ?

duced to aggravate the pride of Edom: "Whereas I made thee small
and despised, by the narrow territory which I assigned to thee, and the
low place I gave thee among the nations of the earth, the pride of thine
heart hath deceived thee," &c. As a fact the Edomites had at this time
acquired very considerable territory, and were a strong and formidable
nation. If that had not been so, what need would there have been to
summon "the nations" to chastise them ?

3. *the clefts of the rock*] The word rock may here be a proper
name, Selah or Petra ; the reference would then be to the rock-hewn
dwellings of that remarkable city. Perhaps, however, the reference is
more general to the "clefts of the rock" which abounded and were
used as habitations throughout Edom proper. The expression which
occurs here and in Jeremiah xlix. 16, is only found beside in Song of
Solomon ii. 14, where it is used of the hiding-place of a dove.

Ewald renders this verse : "Thy heart's haughtiness deceived thee,
who inhabiteth in rock-clefts, his proud dwelling, who saith in his
heart, who shall cast me down to the earth ?"

"The great strength of a position such as Selah's was shewn during
the war of the Independence of Greece, in the case of the monastery of
Megaspelion, which was situated, like Selah, on the face of a precipice.
Ibrahim Pasha was unable to *bring* its defenders *down* by assault from
below, or above, and though ungarrisoned it baffled his utmost efforts."
Speaker's *Commentary*.

For a description of Petra and the approach to it, see note A,
page 40.

4. *thou exalt thyself*] There is no need to supply the word "thyself," as is done by A.V. and others ("though thou wentest as high as
the eagle." Ewald). "Thy nest" is the subject of both clauses. The
words as they stand give a perfectly clear sense in English, as in
Hebrew : **though thou exaltest as the eagle, and though among the
stars thou settest thy nest.** Comp. Num. xxiv. 21, Hab. ii. 9.

5, 6. The completeness of the destruction and desolation of Edom is
depicted by a double contrast. Two cases are supposed in which something would be left behind. The thief or the robber would take his fill

>   If the grape-gatherers came to thee,
>   Would they not leave *some* grapes?
> 6   How are *the things of* Esau searched out!
>   *How* are his hid things sought up!
> 7   All the men of thy confederacy have brought thee *even* to
>   the border:

and depart: the grape-gatherer would not strip every cluster from the vine. But the enemies of Edom would do worse than either of these. They would spare nothing, nor stay their hand till they had left her utterly desolate and bare.

how art thou cut off] These words are an exclamation of the prophet, forced from him by the utter devastation which in prophetic vision he sees before his eyes. *This* is no work of the common robber, of the ordinary spoiler!

6. *the things of Esau*] lit. *how are they searched out, Esau;* i.e. everything, people and property alike, that belongs to Esau.

his hidden things] rather **places**; his treasure-houses and receptacles hewn in the secret places of the rocks, and inaccessible as he thought them. Comp. Jer. xlix. 10. *Hidden treasures*, R.V.

7. The general drift of this verse is plain. It introduces another particular in which the pride of Edom had deceived her. Her trust in the wisdom of her policy, in the sagacious alliances which she had formed, should fail her no less signally than her confidence in the natural security of her position. But the details of the verse, as regards both the alliances referred to and the meaning of some of the expressions used, are not without difficulty.

the men of thy confederacy] As regards the first of these points, the majority of commentators understand by "the men of thy confederacy," "the men that were at peace with thee," neighbouring nations, "probably Moab and Ammon, Tyre and Zidon" (Pusey); or, "Arabian tribes" (Speaker's *Comm.*). But there is reason to believe that the Edomites shared a common fate with the Moabites and Ammonites at the hands of the Chaldean invader, when after the destruction of Jerusalem he was pushing his way towards Egypt. (See Introd. § 3, comp. Ezek. xxv.) It is of course possible that the Edomites were the first to suffer, and that when Nebuchadnezzar came upon them they were deserted and betrayed by their neighbours and allies in the manner described in this verse. But it is at least worthy of consideration (it is a view which Calvin appears to assume as a matter of course) whether the Chaldeans themselves are not intended by "the men of thy confederacy," "the men that were at peace with thee," of whom the prophet speaks. Well might Edom plume himself upon the "understanding" which led him, on the approach of Nebuchadnezzar towards Judea, to make alliance with him, and thus to seize an opportunity of at once venting his ancient spite upon Israel, and securing himself against the attack of the invader. But the wisdom of this astute policy should prove in the issue to be foolishness. It should justify and call

The men that were at peace with thee have deceived thee,
and prevailed against thee ;
They that eat thy bread have laid a wound under thee :

forth on the part of the beholder the exclamation, "There is no understanding in him!" The Chaldean should use Edom for his purpose, and
then take and destroy him in his own craftiness.

have brought thee even to the border] This has been taken to mean
that the neighbouring nations, thy allies, to whom thou sentest for help
in thy time of need, have conducted back to the border or frontier thy
ambassadors with all the usual marks of respect, but have courteously
declined to render thee assistance. The words, however, may mean,
have "driven thee out," R.V. margin (as in Gen. iii. 23, 1 Kings
ix. 7, Isaiah l. 1, where the same verb is used), and may refer to
the Chaldeans. This meaning is given to them by some commentators who understand the reference to be to neighbouring tribes, who
are thus described, they think, as not merely refusing aid to Edom,
but taking active part with the Chaldeans against him.

prevailed against thee] This may mean prevailed against thee in
counsel, outwitted thee, but it is simpler to take it of actual violence
and physical compulsion.

they that eat thy bread have laid a wound under thee] The words,
"they that eat" are not in the Hebrew. Many commentators connect
them with the preceding clause, an arrangement which the order
of the words in the original facilitates : *they have prevailed against
thee, the men of thy peace, of thy bread,* i.e. the men who were
at peace with thee and who ate thy bread. But it is better to
take the clause, "thy bread they make a wound (or a net) under thee,"
separately, and to understand it to mean that thy allies and confederates make thy bread which they eat (and the sacred obligation
according to Eastern ideas of eating bread together must not here be
lost sight of), or thy table at which they sit, an occasion to deal thee
a secret and deadly wound, or to catch thee as it were in the snare of
their insidious plots against thee. If the rendering "snare" be adopted,
and it seems on the whole preferable, the passage receives elucidation
from the words of the Psalmist (lxix. 22) :

> "Let their table before them become a snare,
>   And when they are in peace (let it be) a trap;"

of which "perhaps the meaning may be : let them be like persons who
while sitting at their meals 'in peace,' in security, unarmed, and
unsuspecting, are suddenly surprised by their enemies. Their 'table
becomes a snare,' as exposing them to certain destruction." Dean
Perowne, *on the Psalms*. The whole verse may then be paraphrased :
"Thy confederates, the Chaldeans with whom thou didst enter into
treaty, have driven thee to the border of thy country on every side, and
expelled thee totally from it. Those that were at peace with thee have
treated thee with mingled treachery and violence. The Chaldeans
whom thou regardedst as friends have deceived thee, and prevailed

There is none understanding in him.

8 Shall I not in that day, saith the LORD,
Even destroy the wise *men* out of Edom,
And understanding out of the mount of Esau?

9 And thy mighty *men*, O Teman, shall be dismayed,
To the end that every one of the mount of Esau may be
cut off by slaughter.

against thee. Thy bread which they ate, they have used as a snare to
entrap thee, taking advantage of the friendly relations which existed to
work thy unlooked-for ruin. There is no understanding in him! To
think that the vaunted penetration of Edom should have betrayed him
into so humiliating and complete an overthrow!"

8, 9. Though thus shamefully betrayed and utterly spoiled, the
Edomites might yet possibly have recovered themselves, if those inherent
qualities in which the strength of nations as of individuals consists, had
still been left to them. But the judgment of God would deprive them
of these, and so render their case hopeless. Wisdom and courage, the
two great resources of a nation in adversity, would alike fail them.
Comp. Jerem. xlix. 7, 22.

8. *destroy the wise men*] i.e. so deprive them of their wisdom that
they shall cease to be wise men. Comp. Jer. xlix. 7, "Concerning
Edom, thus saith the Lord of hosts; Is wisdom no more in Teman? is
counsel perished from the prudent? is their wisdom vanished?" There
is perhaps a reference to wisdom as a special characteristic of the
Edomites. " Eliphaz, the chief of Job's friends, the representative of
human wisdom, was a Temanite." (Pusey, see Job ii. 11.) In the
Book of Baruch the Edomites are referred to as types of wisdom. "It
hath not been heard of in Chanaan, neither hath it been seen in Theman.
The Agarenes that seek wisdom upon earth, the merchants of Meran
and of Theman, the authors of fables, and searchers out of understanding;
none of these have known the way of wisdom, or remember her paths."
Baruch iii. 22, 23.

9. *by slaughter*] i.e. by slaughter inflicted on them by their enemies.
This is the simplest and most natural meaning. It might be rendered,
as the same preposition is at the beginning of the next verse, "for," i.e.
on account of and in retribution of the slaughter which the Edomites
had inflicted on the Jews. This clause would then be an introduction
to the following verses, in which the cause of their calamity is treated of
at length. Ewald's rendering, "without battle," though grammatically
possible, is contradicted by Ezekiel xxxv. 8.

10—14. THE CAUSE OF EDOM's DESTRUCTION.

The scene changes. Another picture of violence and cruelty now
rises before the prophet's eyes. He sees Jerusalem encompassed by
enemies and overcome. Strangers carry away captive her forces,
foreigners enter into her gates. And there, not only standing aside in
unbrotherly neutrality, but exulting with malicious joy, speaking words

10—14. *The cause of Edom's destruction.*

For *thy* violence against thy brother Jacob shame shall 10
cover thee,
And thou shalt be cut off for ever.
In the day that thou stoodest on the other side,　　　　11

of proud scorn, doing acts of robbery and wrong, are seen the Edomites. The two pictures, one of the past, the other of the future, he is commissioned to portray before the eyes of men, and to reveal the hidden link that binds them together in the relationship of cause and effect. *v.* 10 contains a general statement of the sin and its punishment. In *vv.* 11—14 the prophet writes in the impassioned strain of a spectator and describes at length the sin. The punishment is further described in *vv.* 15, 16.

10. *Thy brother Jacob*] This was the great aggravation of the violence. "Thou shalt not abhor an Edomite, for he is thy brother," was the command of God to the Jews (Deut. xxiii. 7). Treachery from friends and allies was the meet punishment of such a sin.

thou shalt be cut off for ever] As the sin of Edom is concisely expressed in this verse by the one word violence, the details of that violence being afterwards given, so the punishment of Edom is here proclaimed in its ultimate completeness, the steps of his total extinction being in like manner afterwards described.

11. *In the day that thou stoodest*] lit. *in the day of thy standing*. Nothing can certainly be decided from the language of this and the following verses, as to whether the conduct here ascribed to the Edomites was a thing of the past when Obadiah wrote, or was still future. The phrase "in the day of thy standing" obviously determines nothing as to time; nor does the phrase at the end of this verse, "thou, as one of them," in itself considered. In verse 12 the only grammatical rendering is, "do not look," instead of "thou shouldest not have looked," and the same is true of all the similar expressions in *vv.* 12—14. In this 11th verse two past tenses do indeed occur: "foreigners *entered into* his gates, and *cast* lots upon Jerusalem." And the use of these might be held to favour what is the most natural and obvious impression conveyed by the whole passage, viz. that the prophet is describing a past event. But inasmuch as his description may relate to a prophetic vision which had been vouchsafed to him, and not to an actual scene which he had witnessed, the time indicated remains uncertain, and the question of date must be decided on other grounds. (See Introd. § 11.)

on the other side] comp. Psalm xxxviii. 11 [Heb. 12]. "My lovers and my friends stand aloof from my sore," where the Hebrew expression is the same. It may however be a charge of direct opposition rather than of culpable neutrality. The same expression occurs in this sense in 2 Sam. xviii. 13, "Thou thyself wouldest have set thyself against me." Comp. Daniel x. 13, "withstood me," lit. "stood over against me," where the Hebrew phrase is similar.

In the day that the strangers carried away captive his
  forces,
And foreigners entered *into* his gates,
And cast lots upon Jerusalem,
Even thou *wast* as one of them.

12 But thou shouldest not have looked on the day of thy
  brother in the day that he became a stranger;

strangers, foreigners] This therefore cannot refer to the defeat of
Amaziah by Jehoash. (See Introd. § 11.)

his forces] If this rendering be adopted it will mean, not so much the
army which fled with the king and was overtaken and scattered
(2 Kings xxv. 4, 5), as the bulk of the people, who formed the strength
of the nation and who were carried captive, leaving only the "poor of
the land" behind. (2 Kings xxv. 11, 12; Jer. xxxix. 9, 10.) In this
sense the same Hebrew word is rendered "host" in *v.* 20 below. The
rendering of the margin, and of R.V., "carried away his substance," is
supported by *v.* 13, where the word evidently means substance or wealth.

cast lots upon Jerusalem] i.e. divided its spoil and captives by lot.
Comp. Joel iii. 3 [Heb. iv. 3]; Nahum iii. 10.

thou, as one of them] "thou," the brother, and that too in dark contrast to Samaria the alien. "In the remains of the population of the
Samaritan kingdom it is affecting to see that all sense of ancient rivalry
was lost in the grief of the common calamity. Pilgrims from the
ancient capitals of Ephraim, Samaria, Shechem, and Shiloh came flock-
ing with shorn beards, gashed faces, torn clothes, and loud wailings, to
offer incense on the ruined Temple, which was not their own."
Stanley. (Jer. xli. 5).

12. *Thou shouldest not have looked...have rejoiced...have spoken*]
rather, **look not, rejoice not, speak not.** In this verse it is the
neutrality of Edom, spoken of as "standing on the other side" in the
former part of verse 11, that is condemned. In *vv.* 13, 14 his active co-
operation with the enemy, his being "as one of them," is denounced.
But in both cases there is a climax. In this verse the complacent
looking on deepens into malicious joy, and malicious joy finds expression
in derisive mockery. In the following verses, he who before had stood
afar, draws near, "enters into the gate" with the victorious foe, "looks
on the affliction," as a close spectator of all its horrors, "lays hands on
the spoil," does not scruple to take part in the pillage of his brother,
nor even to waylay the fugitives and deliver them up into the hand of
the enemy. "He dehorts them from malicious rejoicing at their
brother's fall, first in look, then in word, then in act, in covetous participation of the spoil, and lastly in murder." Pusey.

looked on the day] Comp. "the day of Jerusalem." Ps. cxxxvii. 7.
"Malicious gazing on human calamity, forgetful of man's common
origin, and common liability to ill, is the worst form of human hate.
It was one of the contumelies of the Cross, *They gaze, they look* with joy
upon Me. Psalm xxii. 17." Pusey.

Neither shouldest thou have rejoiced over the children of
Judah in the day of their destruction;
Neither shouldest thou have spoken proudly in the day
of distress.
Thou shouldest not have entered into the gate of my 13
people in the day of their calamity:
Yea, thou shouldest not have looked on their affliction in
the day of their calamity,
Nor have laid *hands* on their substance in the day of their
calamity;
Neither shouldest thou have stood in the crossway, to cut 14
off those of his that did escape;
Neither shouldest thou have delivered up those of his
that did remain in the day of distress.
For the day of the LORD *is* near upon all the heathen: 15

became a stranger] i.e. was treated as a stranger, cruelly and unjustly:
or was made a stranger by being carried into captivity. The clause
however may mean "in the day of his calamity," or "disaster," R.V.
rejoiced] "He that is glad at calamities shall not be unpunished."
Prov. xvii. 5.
spoken proudly] lit. "make thy mouth great" in derision and
mockery. This may refer either to proud boastful words, or to mock-
ing grimaces and contortions of the mouth.
  13. *Thou shouldest not have entered...looked...laid hands*] rather,
enter not, look not, lay not hands.
  The gate of my people] i.e. the city of Jerusalem, comp. "he is come
unto the gate of my people, even to Jerusalem." Micah i. 9. The emphatic "thou also," thou the brother as well as they the aliens, follows
the word "look" in the Hebrew, though it is unnoticed in A. V., "look
not thou also on his affliction." "If other neighbours do it, yet do thou
abstain, seeing thou art of one blood. If thou canst not render assistance, at least shew some sign of sorrow and sympathy." Calvin.
  14. *Neither shouldest thou have stood...delivered up*] rather, **stand
not, deliver not up.**
  15, 16. After the description in *vv.* 11—14, of the fault for which
Edom was to be punished, the prophet returns in these two verses to the
subject of *vv.* 2—9, and completes the description of the punishment
that should be inflicted on him. He connects them by the word "for,"
at once with the prediction of *v.* 10, "thou shalt be cut off for ever,"
and with the earnest dissuasions of the verses that have followed.
  15. *The day of the Lord*] The order of the words, "for near is the
day of the Lord," accords with the fact that the day of the Lord is here
spoken of as something already known and familiar. It was first
revealed to the prophet Joel (i. 15; ii. 1, 31 [Heb, iii. 4]). There as
here it had reference first to some nearer typical visitation and judg-

As thou hast done, it shall be done unto thee;
Thy reward shall return upon thine own head.

16 For as ye have drunk upon my holy mountain,
So shall all the heathen drink continually,
Yea, they shall drink, and they shall swallow down,
And they shall be as though they had not been.

ment, but included the great final day into which the prophet's view
here expands.

as thou hast done] comp. Ezekiel xxxv. 15 and Psalm cxxxvii. 8.

thy reward] rather, **thy work**; *dealing*, R.V. Comp. Joel iii. 7
[Heb., iv. 7].

As ye have drunk] This is commonly interpreted to mean, "As ye
Edomites have drunk in triumphant revelry and carousal on my holy
mountain, rejoicing with unhallowed joy over its destruction, so shall
(ye and) all the nations drink continually the wine of God's wrath and
indignation." But it is better to understand the first clause as referring
to the Jews: "As ye have drunk (who are) upon my holy mountain;
as even you, who are my chosen people and inhabit the mountain con-
secrated by my presence, have not escaped the cup of my wrath, so all
the nations shall drink of that same cup, not with a passing salutary
draught as you have done, but with a continuous swallowing down, till
they have wrung out the dregs thereof and been brought to nothing by
their consuming power." The "drinking" is thus the same in both
clauses and not as in the other interpretation, literal in the first clause,
and figurative in the second. Thus too the word "continually" has its
proper force, by virtue of the contrast which it suggests between the Jews,
for whom the bitter draught was only temporary, for amendment and not
for destruction, and the heathen who were to drink on till they perished.
And this view of the words is strikingly confirmed by the parallel passages in Jeremiah. To that prophet the commission is given by God,
"Take the wine cup of this fury at mine hand, and cause all the nations
to whom I send thee to drink it." Beginning with "Jerusalem and the
cities of Judah" the prophet passes the cup in turn to Edom. And if
the nations refuse to take the cup, he is to answer them by Obadiah's
argument that even God's holy mountain has not escaped: "ye shall
certainly drink. For do I begin to bring evil on the city which is called
by my name and should ye be utterly unpunished?" (xxv. 15—29).
Again in the chapter in which, as we have seen, Jeremiah has much in
common with Obadiah, he uses the figure of the cup of judgment with
reference both to Jews and Edomites as though he had so understood it
here. "Behold," he says, "they whose judgment was not to drink of
the cup have assuredly drunken, and art thou he that shall altogether go
unpunished?" xlix. 12. And once more in the book of Lamentations
he prophesies, "the cup also (of which we have drunk) shall pass
through unto thee," and then draws, in the following verse, the same
contrast in plain language between the punishment of Israel and of
Edom, which is here drawn by Obadiah by the figure of the single and
the continuous draught. "The punishment of thine iniquity is accom-

17—21.　*The Restoration of Israel.*

But upon mount Zion shall be deliverance, and there 17
  shall be holiness ;
And the house of Jacob shall possess their possessions.
And the house of Jacob shall be a fire,   18
And the house of Joseph a flame,

plished, O daughter of Zion; he will no more carry thee away into captivity. He will visit thine iniquity, O daughter of Edom; he will discover thy sins" (iv. 21, 22).

17—21. THE RESTORATION OF ISRAEL.

By an easy transition the prophet passes to the second and brighter
part of his picture. The destruction of her enemies is accompanied by
the restoration and salvation of Israel. There is however no sudden
break between the two portions of the prophecy. The key-note of
deliverance had already been struck in the earlier portion by the
implied promise (*v.* 16) that the punishment of Israel was not to be,
like that of her enemies, continual. The tones of vengeance are heard
still in the later portion, and are only lost at length in the final strain of
victory, "The kingdom shall be the Lord's." Israel is to regain her
former possessions (*v.* 17), to overcome her ancient foes (*v.* 18), to
spread abroad in all directions (*vv.* 19, 20), till as the ultimate issue
which in the fulness of time shall be reached, God's kingdom is set up
in the world (*v.* 21).

17.　*But upon mount Zion shall be deliverance*] Unlike Edom (*v.* 9)
and the other heathen nations (*v.* 16) whose destruction will be complete,
Israel even in her worst calamities shall have "a deliverance," i. e. remnant of the people, who shall escape destruction and be delivered out of
trouble, to be as it were a fresh nucleus and starting-point of the nation.
The word here rendered "deliverance" occurs in Exodus x. 5, "that
which is escaped," to denote the remnant of the fruits of the earth left
by the plague of hail. It is used in the same sense as here in Isaiah
xxxvii. 31, 32, "that is escaped," "they that escape;" and in Joel ii. 32
[Heb. iii. 5].

there shall be holiness] rather (margin, and R.V.), it (**Mount Zion**) **shall
be holy**, lit. "holiness," comp. Joel iii. 17 [Heb., iv. 17]; Rev. xxi. 27.

their possessions] Not the possessions of Edom and of the heathen—
that is spoken of in the following verses, but their own possessions.
"When the children of Israel shall have returned from exile God will
at the same time restore to them their ancient country, so as for them to
possess whatever had been promised to their father Abraham."
Calvin.

18.　*The house of Jacob...the house of Joseph*] Both are mentioned to
shew that the remnant of the whole nation, not only of the two tribes,
but of the ten, is included. The same names are used to describe the
entire nation in Ps. lxxvii. 15 [Heb. 16]; lxxx. 1 [Heb. 2]; lxxxi. 4, 5
[Heb. 5, 6].

And the house of Esau for stubble,
And they shall kindle in them, and devour them;
And there shall not be *any* remaining of the house of
    Esau;
For the LORD hath spoken *it.*

19   And *they of* the south shall possess the mount of Esau;
And *they of* the plain the Philistines:

any remaining] "a survivor." The punishment here denounced
against Edom is quite distinct from that earlier punishment, of which the
nations are summoned to be the instruments (*vv.* 1, 2). It is that final
destruction, which they suffered at the hands of Jews only, first of Judas
Maccabæus, and then, in their total extermination, of John Hyrcanus.
See Introduction, § III.

19, 20. Restored to their own land, the Jews shall extend their territory in all directions, and shall realise the promise made to their father
Jacob, "Thou shalt spread abroad to the west, and to the east, and to
the north, and to the south." Gen. xxviii. 14. The two tribes, Judah
and Benjamin, as the sole remaining representatives of the people of God
in the prophet's time, are alone directly mentioned by him in the distribution of the land. But the ten tribes are not thereby excluded from a
share in the returning prosperity of the nation. See note on *v.* 18. In
v. 19 the exiles who returned from Babylon are provided for. The
whole country on the west of the Jordan is assigned to Judah, and Benjamin takes possession of Gilead on the east side. In *v.* 20, other Jewish
exiles in Phœnicia and elsewhere are remembered, and a place found
for them in the conquered territory of Esau.

19. *they of the south*] lit. **the south.** This is the first of the three
divisions of the tribe of Judah, in the original apportionment of the land
by Joshua: "the tribe of the children of Judah, toward the coast of
Edom *southward*" (i.e. in the direction of the "Negeb," or hot, dry
country, which formed the southern frontier. *Sinai and Palestine*,
pp. 159, 160). Joshua xv. 21. The restored exiles of Judah shall not
only possess again this their ancient domain; but whereas it was before
"too much for them," so that "the children of Simeon had their
inheritance within the inheritance of them" (Josh. xix. 9), now they
shall not only occupy it, but spreading still further southward shall
"possess the mount of Esau."

they of the plain] *Shephelah: the low-land*, R.V. This is the second
of the original divisions of Judah. (Josh. xv. 33, where the same
Hebrew word is translated "valley.") It is the great maritime plain
along the western coast of Palestine. See *Sinai and Palestine*, chap. VI.
pp. 255, seq. This again was not only to be repossessed, but its ancient
boundaries were to be overpassed, and the entire country of the
Philistines, to the shores of the Mediterranean, was to be won for
Judah.

And they shall possess the fields of Ephraim, and the
fields of Samaria :
And Benjamin *shall possess* Gilead.
And the captivity of this host of the children of Israel *shall* 20
possess that of the Canaanites, *even* unto Zarephath ;

and they shall possess]   The subject of this clause may of course be
the two divisions of Judah, "they of the south," and "they of the
plain," already mentioned.   But it is much better to suppose that the
prophet here refers to the remainder of the tribe, who are spoken of as
"in the mountains" (Josh. xv. 48).   "And they (the tribe of Judah, i.e.
the remaining portion of them) shall possess" the remaining portion of
Palestine proper, the country of the ten tribes, "the field of Ephraim
and the field of Samaria."

and Benjamin shall possess Gilead]   Judah having thus acquired the
whole country on that side Jordan, Benjamin, the only other tribe now
under consideration, takes possession of the territory which once belonged to the two tribes and a half on the other side.

20.   Two ways of rendering this verse are given in our English
Bibles, one in the text, the other in the margin.   The latter of these
fully expressed would be :   " *And the captivity of this host of the children
of Israel shall possess that* (i.e. the land) *of the Canaanites, even unto
Zarephath ; and the captivity of Jerusalem shall possess that which is in
Sepharad ; they shall possess the cities of the south.*"   But a third
rendering of the verse is possible and appears to be more satisfactory
than either of these :—"**And the captivity of this host of the children
of Israel which the Canaanites (have carried captive) even unto
Zarephath and the captivity of Jerusalem which is in Sepharad (these)
shall possess the cities of the south.**"   The prophet having assigned their dwelling-place to the main body of the people, the tribes
of Judah and Benjamin who returned from Babylon, now bethinks him
of their brethren, who in the general disruption of the Chaldean invasion
had been carried captive in other directions.   He mentions two such
bodies of captives, whether as including or as representing all Jews who
were in such a case, and for them he finds a home in the regions of the
south.   Another rendering is adopted in R.V.

this host of the children of Israel]   It is suggested in the Speaker's
Commentary, that the word " this" here " indicates the body (of exiles)
to which Obadiah himself belonged, and of which he formed one.   We
know nothing," it is said, " of Obadiah's history ; he may well have
been one of the many inhabitants of Judah who had to flee before the
Babylonish inroad, and were afterwards spread as homeless exiles
through the cities of Palestine and Phœnicia.   If this be so, a touching
personal interest attaches itself to the prophet's words.   He comforts
his brother-exiles in Canaan by telling them that they, as well as the
exiles in Sepharad, should return, and take possession of the cities of
the south."   The suggestion is interesting, but it is more natural to
understand the expression, "this host of the children of Israel," of the

And the captivity of Jerusalem, which *is* in Sepharad,
Shall possess the cities of the south.

21 And saviours shall come up on mount Zion to judge the
mount of Esau ;

entire body of the Jews, uprooted and doomed to exile as Obadiah saw
them when he wrote. Of this whole captive host, he says, that portion
which has been carried into Phœnicia shall be thus provided for. In
this sense the word "host" ("forces") is perhaps used in verse 11. See
note there.

even unto Zarephath] The *Sarepta* of the New Testament (Luke
iv. 26) famous in the history of Elijah, 1 Kings xvii. 9—24. It was a
considerable town, as its ruins now shew, on the coast road between
Tyre and Sidon. Its modern representative, Sarafend, is a small village
on the hill above.

in Sepharad] Great difference of opinion exists as to the meaning and
reference of this word. The conjecture of Jerome that it is not a proper
name, but the Assyrian word for "boundary," which the prophet has
adopted, is accepted by some. It would then mean, "who are scattered abroad in all the boundaries and regions of the earth." Comp.
James i. 1. It is more probable, however, that like Zarephath in the
other clause of the verse, Sepharad is the name of a place, though it is
not easy to determine what place is intended by it. The modern Jews
understand it of Spain, and accordingly, "at the present day the
Spanish Jews, who form the chief of the two great sections into which
the Jewish nation is divided, are called by the Jews themselves the
Sephardim, German Jews being known as the *Ashkenazim*." *Dict. of
the Bible*, Art. *Sepharad*. By others it is identified with Sardis, the
capital of the Lydian kingdom, the name having been discovered as it is
thought to designate Sardis in the cuneiform Persian inscriptions.
Adopting this view (for which some have found support in Joel iii. 6),
Dr Pusey thus explains the whole verse : "Zarephath (probably 'smelt-
ing-house,' and so a place of slave-labour, pronounced Sarepta in
St Luke) belonged to Sidon, lying on the sea about half way between it
and Tyre. These were then, probably, captives, placed by the Tyrians
for the time in safe keeping in the narrow plain between Lebanon and
the sea, intercepted by Tyre itself from their home, and awaiting to be
transported to a more distant slavery. These, with those already sold
to the Grecians and in slavery at Sardis, form one whole. They stand
as representatives of all who, whatever their lot, had been rent off from
the Lord's land, and had been outwardly severed from His heritage."
Other conjectures are given in the article in the *Dictionary of the Bible*.
Whatever uncertainty attaches to the word *Sepharad*, the drift of the
prophecy is perfectly clear, viz. that not only the exiles from Babylon,
but Jewish captives from other and distant regions shall be brought back
to live prosperously within the enlarged borders of their own land.

21. *saviours*] i.e. *deliverers*. The word, enshrined already in the
name of Joshua, the great deliverer, is frequently applied to the Judges :

And the kingdom shall be the LORD's.

"The Lord raised up judges, which delivered (saved) them out of the hand of those that spoiled them." Judges ii. 16. "Thou gavest them saviours, who saved them out of the hand of their enemies." Nehem. ix. 27. See also Judges ii. 18; iii. 31; vi. 14, 15, 36. It is applied once in the later history to king Joash, as the deliverer of Israel from the oppression of the Syrians: "the Lord gave Israel a saviour." 2 Kings xiii. 5 with 25. Here the immediate reference is to the Maccabees and such like human saviours. But as the long lines of Jewish prophets, and priests, and kings were respectively the manifold types of the one true Prophet, Priest, and King, so their saviours fore-shadowed Him, of whom in the fulness of time it was said, "Unto you is born in the city of David a Saviour," and whom, as "a Saviour," His Church still looks for. (Philipp. iii. 20; Heb. ix. 28.)

to judge the mount of Esau] The vengeance on Esau, which is the predominant idea of this short prophecy, is still before the prophet's mind. And yet perhaps we may say that that wider sense of "judg-ing," which the remembrance of the "judges who judged (i.e. governed) Israel" would suggest, is here prevailing. Esau subdued shall also be incorporated, and share the privileges of that righteous and beneficent rule with which Zion shall be blessed.

the kingdom shall be the Lord's] The grand climax is here certainly, however indistinctly, before the prophet's mind. It is this that stamps the writings of the Hebrew prophets with a character which is all their own, and proves them to be inspired with an inspiration of God, other and higher far than that of the most gifted seers and poets of other lands and ages. With them the national and the human reach forth ever to the divine and the universal. The kingdom of Israel gives place to and is lost in the kingdom of God. Never in any adequate realisation even of Jewish idea and conception, could it be said of any period of the history of Israel after the return from Babylon, "The kingdom is the Lord's." Never of any country or any church, much less of the world at large, has so great a word been true, since in the person and the religion of Christ the kingdom of God has come among us. Still the Church prays as for a thing still future, "Thy kingdom come." Still Obadiah's last note of prophecy, "the kingdom shall be the Lord's," vibrates on, till at last it shall be taken up into the great chorus of accomplished hope and satisfied expectation, "Hallelujah! for the Lord God Omnipotent reigneth."

THE following graphic description of Petra from the pen of the late Dean Stanley, is taken by permission of the publishers from his well-known work, *Sinai and Palestine:*—

"You descend from those wide downs and those white cliffs which I have before described as forming the background of the Red City when seen from the west, and before you opens a deep cleft between rocks of red sandstone rising perpendicularly to the height of one, two, or three hundred feet. This is the *Sîk,* or 'cleft;' through this flows—if one may use the expression - the dry torrent, which, rising in the mountains half-an-hour hence, gives the name by which alone Petra is now known amongst the Arabs—Wâdy Mûsa. 'For,'—so Sheykh Mohammed tells us—'as surely as Jebel Hârûn (the Mountain of Aaron) is so called from the burial-place of Aaron, is Wâdy Mûsa (the Valley of Moses) so called from the cleft being made by the rod of Moses when he brought the stream through into the valley beyond.' It is, indeed, a place worthy of the scene, and one could long to believe it. Follow me, then, down this magnificent gorge—the most magnificent, beyond all doubt, which I have ever beheld. The rocks are almost precipitous, or rather, they would be, if they did not, like their brethren in all this region, overlap, and crumble, and crack, as if they would crash over you. The gorge is about a mile and a half long, and the opening of the cliffs at the top is throughout almost as narrow as the narrowest part of the defile of Pfeffers, which, in dimensions and form, it more resembles than any other of my acquaintance. At its very first entrance you pass under the arch which, though greatly broken, still spans the chasm—meant apparently to indicate the approach to the city. You pass under this along the bed of the torrent, now rough with stones, but once a regular paved road like the Appian Way, the pavement still remaining at intervals in the bed of the stream—the stream, meanwhile, which now has its own wild way, being then diverted from its course along troughs hewn in the rock above, or conducted through earthenware pipes, still traceable. These, and a few niches for statues now gone, are the only traces of human hand. What a sight it must have been, when all these were perfect! A road, level and smooth, running through these tremendous rocks, and the blue sky just visible above, the green caper-plant and wild ivy hanging in festoons over the heads of the travellers as they wind along, the flowering oleander fringing then, as now, this marvellous highway like the border of a garden walk. You move on; and the ravine, and with it the road,—and with the road in old times the caravans of India,—winds as if it were the most flexible of rivers, instead of being in truth a rent through a mountain wall. In this respect, in its sinuosity, it differs from any other like gorge I ever saw. The peculiarity is, perhaps, occasioned by the singularly friable character of the cliffs, the same character that has caused the thousand excavations beyond; and the effect is, that instead of the uniform character of most ravines, you are constantly turning round corners, and catching new lights and new aspects, in which to view the cliffs themselves. They are, for the most part, deeply red, and when you see their tops emerging from the shade and glowing in the sunshine I could almost forgive the exaggeration that calls them scarlet. But in fact they are of the darker hues which in the shadow amount almost to black, and such is their colour at the point to which I have brought you, after a mile or more through the defile—the cliffs overarching in their narrowest contraction—when, suddenly through the narrow opening left between the two dark walls of another turn of the gorge, you see a pale pink front of pillars and sculptured figures closing your view from top to bottom. You rush towards it, you find yourself at the end of the defile, and in the presence of an excavated temple, which remains almost entirely perfect between the two flanks of dark rock out of which it is hewn; its preservation and its peculiarly light and rosy tint being alike due to its singular position facing the ravine or rather wall of rock, through which the ravine issues, and thus sheltered beyond any other building (if one may so call it) from the wear-and-tear of weather, which has effaced, though not defaced, the features, and tanned the complexion of all the other temples.

This I only saw by degrees, coming upon it from the west; but to the travellers of old times, and to those who, like Burckhardt in modern times, came down the defile, not knowing what they were to see, and meeting with this as the first image of the Red City, I cannot conceive anything more striking. There is nothing of peculiar grace or grandeur in the temple itself—(the Khazné, or Treasury, it is called)—it is of the most debased style of Roman architecture; but under the circumstances, I almost think one is more startled by finding in these wild and impracticable mountains a production of the last effort of a decaying and over-refined civilisation, than if it were something which, by its better and simpler taste, mounted more nearly to the source where Art and Nature were one.

Probably anyone who entered Petra this way, would be so electrified by this apparition (which I cannot doubt to have been evoked there purposely, as you would place a fountain or an obelisk at the end of an avenue), as to have no eyes to behold or sense to appreciate anything else. Still, I must take you to the end. The Sik, though it opens here, yet contracts once more, and it is in this last stage that those red and purple variegations, which I have before described, appear in their most gorgeous hues; and here also begins, what must have been properly the Street of Tombs, the Appian Way of Petra. Here they are most numerous, the rock is honeycombed with cavities of all shapes and sizes, and through these you advance till the defile once more opens, and you see—strange and unexpected sight!—with tombs above, below, and in front, a Greek Theatre hewn out of the rock, its tiers of seats literally red and purple alternately, in the native rock. Once more the defile closes with its excavations, and once more opens in the area of Petra itself; the torrent-bed passing now through absolute desolation and silence, though strewn with the fragments which shew that you once entered on a splendid and busy city gathered along in the rocky banks, as along the quays of some great northern river."

JONAH.

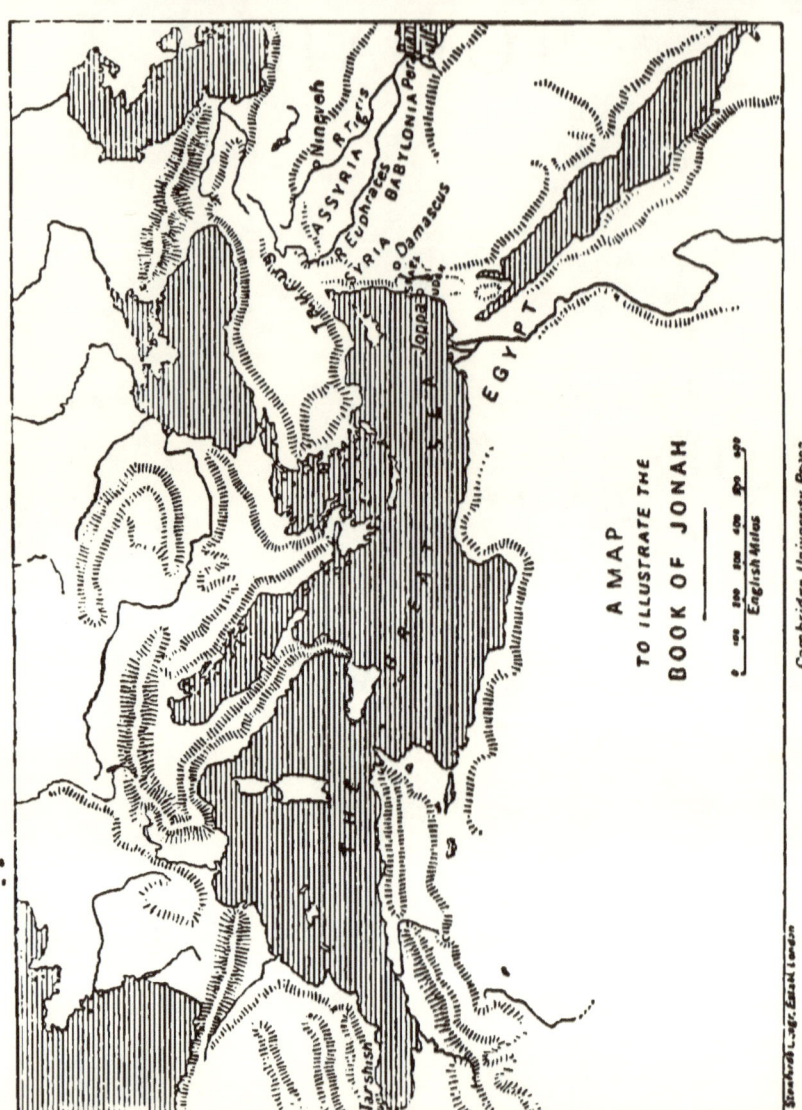

A MAP
TO ILLUSTRATE THE
BOOK OF JONAH

0   100   200   300   400   500   600
English Miles

Cambridge University Press

Nineveh
R. Tigris
ASSYRIA
R. Euphrates
SYRIA
BABYLONIA
Persian
Damascus
Jerusalem
Joppa
THE GREAT SEA
EGYPT
Tarshish

Stanford's Geog. Estab. London

INTRODUCTION.

CHAPTER I.

THE AUTHOR.

1. THERE is no reason to doubt that Jonah was himself the author of the book which bears his name. There is nothing inconsistent with that view in the contents of the book. No other satisfactory theory of authorship has been suggested. The candour of the writer, supposing him to be relating his own history, finds a parallel in the case of other inspired writers both in the Old and New Testaments. The graphic style of the book harmonises with the vigorous and resolute character of Jonah as portrayed in its pages.

2. Of Jonah himself very little is known beyond what we gather from this book. There is however one other mention of him in the Old Testament, which furnishes us with some particulars concerning him. In 2 Kings xiv. 25, we read of Jeroboam II, king of Israel, that "he restored the coast of Israel from the entering of Hamath unto the sea of the plain, according to the word of the Lord God of Israel, which He spake by the hand of His servant Jonah, the son of Amittai, the prophet, which was of Gath-hepher." It can hardly be doubted that the Jonah thus spoken of is the same person as the Jonah of this book. Both are prophets. Both are sons of Amittai. And when it is remembered that neither the name Jonah, nor the name Amittai, occurs anywhere else in the Old Testament, it appears most improbable that there should have been two distinct persons, both prophets, both bearing the same un-

common name, and both sons of a father with the same un-
common name[1].

3. Assuming then, as we may reasonably do, their identity,
we learn from the passage in Kings,

(a) That Jonah was a prophet of the Northern kingdom
(Israel) ;

(b) That his birthplace was Gath-hepher[2], a town of
Lower Galilee, not far from Nazareth, in the tribe of Za-
bulon ;

(c) And that he exercised the prophetical office, either
before the reign of Jeroboam II. or very early in that reign[3].

He would thus be a contemporary of Hosea[4] and Amos[5], if
indeed he was not earlier than they, and therefore one of the
most ancient, if not the most ancient, of the prophets whose
writings we possess.

[1] Jonah means *a dove*, Amittai, *true*. The latter name, which is
thought by some to be identical with Matthew, has given rise to the
tradition that Jonah was the son of the widow of Zarephath, whom
Elijah raised to life, and on receiving whom at his hands she said,
" Now by this I know that thou art a man of God, and that the word of
the Lord in thy mouth is *truth*," 1 Kings xvii. 24. An equally uncertain
tradition makes him also "the boy who attended Elijah to the wilderness," and "the youth who anointed Jehu."

[2] Called Gittah-hepher, Josh. xix. 13. It is in all probability the
same as the modern village of el-Meshhad, where by a constant tradition
from the time of Jerome to the present day, the tomb of Jonah is
pointed out. See Smith's *Bib. Dict.* Art. *Gath-hepher*, and Pusey
Commentary on Jonah, Introd. p. 1.

[3] Ewald writes: " It follows clearly from the words in 2 Kings xiv.
25—27 that this Jonah uttered the prediction neither long before nor
long after the accession of Jeroboam II., especially as the king, according to all appearance, won his great victories very early. Jonah's prediction therefore must fall in with the childhood of Jeroboam or in
the first commencement of his reign." *Hist. of Israel*, vol. iv. p. 124,
note 1. Carpenter's Translation. According to the ordinary chronology
Jeroboam's reign was from B.C. 823 to B.C. 782.

[4] Hosea i. 1.   [5] Amos i. 1.

CHAPTER II.

IIISTORICAL CHARACTER OF THE BOOK.

1. The thoughtful student of the book of Jonah cannot fail to observe that it differs in some important particulars from the other prophetical writings of the Old Testament.

(*a*) In form it is a story and not a prophecy. It is an account of what befell a prophet, and not a record of his predictions.

(*b*) In style it is almost dramatic. Its teaching, whatever it may be, is rather acted before our eyes than uttered for our ears.

(*c*) Moreover, the miraculous or supernatural element enters in an unusual degree into the contents of this book. Seldom, if ever, do we find so many and so great wonders accumulated in the compass of so brief a narrative.

The question has accordingly been raised, whether this book is not rather to be regarded as an allegory or parable or romance, either founded on fact, or altogether independent of any real basis, than as a history of what actually happened.

2. It can hardly be doubted that this question really owes its origin to the miraculous character of the book of Jonah. Amongst the principal advocates of the non-historical theory of the book are those who deny the possibility of miracles. With a marvellous amount of ingenuity, but with an entire want of agreement among themselves, these writers have proposed a great variety of interpretations of the book of Jonah, including even the suggestion, of which it would be difficult to say whether it be more improbable or more irreverent, that it

is to be regarded as a Jewish adaptation of a heathen mythical legend[1].

3. Without going however to any such lengths as these, without doubting the possibility of miracles, or denying the canonicity and inspiration of the book of Jonah, it may still be open to us to consider the question of its historical character. May it not be, we may ask, all that the most devout Christian holds it to be, and yet be not a history, but a divinely originated parable or allegory?

4. To the question thus modified it may be objected in reply, that even in this form it is really suggested by the miracles with which this book abounds. But for them, it may well be doubted whether anyone would ever have taken the book of Jonah to be anything but history. Are then the miracles, for into this the enquiry resolves itself, really such as to warrant the question? We think not. When fairly examined they lose much of that character of the merely marvellous, which to a cursory and mistaken view they have some of them appeared to wear. By such probable explanations as will be given of each of them in its place below, they may be brought properly within the sphere of the Gospel miracles themselves, as being for the most part accelerations and adaptations of the known powers and processes of nature, the normal, if extraordinary working, as Holy Scripture reveals it to us, of a living and ever-present God. And if this be so, then the question falls to the ground together with the supposed necessity for asking it.

5. But even were it otherwise, were there anything in these pages which when rightly explained lay beyond the sphere of humble and intelligent faith, are we really gainers by transferring them from the region of history to that of parable or allegory? It is not the wont of the sacred writers to make use of portents or prodigies in their allegorical or parabolic teaching. It is

---

[1] The story of Perseus and Andromeda, in one or other of its forms or modifications. The whole theory is fully stated and as fully refuted by Dr Pusey, Introduction to *Commentary on Jonah*, pp. 261—263.

one of the recognised distinctions between canonical and apocryphal writings, that whilst the latter often abound in legends and marvels, the former never transgress the limits of the possible, even in their figurative teaching. Even from a literary point of view, higher considerations apart, the allegorical character of the book of Jonah cannot be satisfactorily maintained. On that hypothesis it is out of harmony as a whole. What may be called the setting of the allegory is too exact, too detailed, too closely in accordance with facts, to be in keeping with the allegory itself. The book is composed of two elements which will not properly fuse together. One whole section of it at least, Jonah's psalm of thanksgiving in the second chapter, is quite out of place. Most pertinent in a true history, it becomes in an allegory a discord and an intrusion.

6. Nor is it easy to understand why the writer of an allegory, free to choose his characters at will, should have selected a known prophet of God as the subject of so great misconduct and reprobation. If the introduction of a prophet were necessary, to heighten the contrast and to enforce the moral of his teaching, would not that end have equally been answered by a fictitious name, or by the omission of the name altogether? If Jonah did not act as this book represents him to have done, it is incredible that a Jewish writer should have ascribed conduct such as this to him, and that the fiction in which he ascribed it should have found a place in the Jewish Canon. This consideration is fatal to such a theory of the origin of the book of Jonah, as that which has been proposed by a recent commentator[1]. He supposes the book to be in form a kind of historical romance, written long after the time of Jonah, and founded either upon a tradition which credited Jonah "with a missionary journey to distant and powerful Nineveh," or upon a "real fact," a political "legation from the king of Israel to the king of Assyria," which however this later writer was unable to conceive of, except under a religious aspect, the moral re-

---

[1] Kalisch, *Bible Studies*, Part II, pp. 122, 123, 133, 134.

formation of the Assyrians to whom Jonah was sent. But when, in pursuit of this arbitrary theory, he comes to deal with the "ill-feeling" exhibited by Jonah, and asks, "Was the author justified in imputing to an old and honoured prophet such bitterness, nay, such meanness?" he has no better answer than this to give, "we must, therefore, ascribe that feature to the author himself, who thus wronged both his hero and his composition."

7. There remains however another argument for the historical character of the book of Jonah, which is the weightiest of all, and which would to a Christian mind appear to be of itself conclusive. In a well-known passage in the Gospels our Lord makes a double reference to the book of Jonah.

(*a*) To the request for a sign, addressed to Him by the Scribes and Pharisees, He replies, "An evil and adulterous generation seeketh after a sign; and there shall no sign be given to it, but the sign of the prophet Jonas: for as Jonas was three days and three nights in the whale's belly; so shall the Son of man be three days and three nights in the heart of the earth[1]." It is difficult to see how, if Jonah's incarceration in the fish were merely an allegory, it could have been referred to by our Lord in language such as this. The whole Old Testament history not excluding even its minor incidents was, as St Paul teaches us, allegorical[2]; allegorically intended by its divine Author, and to be interpreted allegorically by His Church. But to recognise this is not to invalidate the historical truth of the narrative. It is true history, but representative history; history which foretells throughout Christ and the good things to come. With this view the parallel which our Lord draws between what befell Jonah and what should befall Himself exactly coincides. There is no departure from the firm basis of historical fact on which our holy religion rests; no endangering the literal truth of the second member of the comparison by admitting the unreality of the first.

(*b*) But even if it were conceded that our Lord's

---

[1] Matthew xii. 39, 40.   [2] Galatians iv. 24.

words so far are compatible with the non-historic view, there follow in the same place other words of His, which are plainly repugnant to any such interpretation, "The men of Nineveh," He goes on to say, "shall rise in judgment with this generation, and shall condemn it, because they repented at the preaching of Jonas; and, behold, a greater than Jonas is here[1]." Is it possible to understand a reference like this on the non-historic theory of the book of Jonah? The future Judge is speaking words of solemn warning to those who shall hereafter stand convicted at His bar. Intensely real He would make the scene in anticipation to them, as it was real, as if then present, to Himself. And yet we are to suppose Him to say that imaginary persons who at the imaginary preaching of an imaginary prophet repented in imagination, shall rise up in that day and condemn the actual impenitence of those His actual hearers, that the fictitious characters of a parable shall be arraigned at the same bar with the living men of that generation.

On all these grounds then it would seem that the book of Jonah can only be regarded as actual history.

CHAPTER III.

OBJECT OF THE BOOK.

1. It has been held by some, that the chief object of this book is to teach the nature and efficacy of true repentance. "So obvious," says a recent writer, "is the main idea which pervades the book and stamps it with the character of perfect unity—the idea of the wonderful power of true repentance—that it seems surprising that this point should ever have been mistaken, and should have called forth the most varied and

---

[1] Matthew xii. 41.

most fanciful views[1]." That we have in the book of Jonah two striking examples of repentance and its happy results, one of individual repentance in the case of Jonah himself and of his deliverance and restoration to his office and mission; the other of national repentance in the case of the Ninevites, and that they hold an important place in the moral teaching of the book, is undoubtedly true. The latter of them is thought worthy by our Lord Himself to be singled out from the history of the Old Testament as a typical example of repentance[2]. But to teach repentance is not the main object of this book. To regard it as such is to miss altogether the proper aim and design of the author. It is to leave unexplained the flight of Jonah and his reluctance to be the messenger of mercy to Nineveh. It is practically to expunge the last chapter of the book, and to make its teaching culminate in the words, "And God saw their works, that they turned from their evil way; and God repented of the evil that He had said that He would do unto them; and He did it not[3]." The lesson of repentance is only a part, however important, of the higher and wider lesson which this book is designed to teach us.

2. Still more prominent when we study the book as a whole is the object of the writer to shew in its true colours the unloving exclusiveness which too often characterised the Jew, and to rebuke the grudging narrow-mindedness that would deny all favour from the God of Israel to the Gentile world. It is the spirit of the elder brother in the parable that the author is commissioned to reprove. By that spirit Jonah was actuated, as he himself confesses (c. iv. 2.). It was the source of all that was unworthy in his conduct as here described. It was at the root of his disobedience at the first, and of his subsequent

---

[1] Kalisch, *Bible Studies*, Part II., The Book of Jonah, p. 265.

[2] Matthew xii. 41.

[3] Ch. iii. 10. One of these writers at least is candid enough to confess this consequence of his view. "It may be admitted," says Kalisch, "that if this chapter (iv.) were wanting, it would hardly have been missed, and that, without it, the story would have concluded almost as satisfactorily as it does in its present form."

displeasure. It prompted him to throw up his office as a
prophet, and abandon his privileges as an Israelite, to relinquish
alike the service and the favour of his God, rather than be His
instrument of blessing to a heathen nation. It found vent in
the ungenerous anger and petulant complaints, with which the
unwelcome reprieve of the sentence on Nineveh was received by
him. Taught by the discipline of God to see this spirit in its
true light, he exhibits it (if as is most probable he was himself
the author of this book) in his own personal history, in all its
deformity and injustice, as a lesson to others. He exalts the ·
Gentile in comparison of the Jew. He places the heathen
sailors in the storm in favourable contrast with himself, the
prophet of God, and by implication at least, the penitent
Ninevites in like favourable contrast with impenitent Israel.
With noble disregard of self he is content to pass out of view at
the close of the book silenced and disgraced, that so he may the
better point the moral with which he is charged. Yet not even
this, taken alone and simply in itself considered, is the proper aim
and object of the book of Jonah. Like the teaching of repentance, it is an integral part of a larger aim.

3. Three Acts, as it were, in a drama, three movements, so
to speak, in an oratorio, this book contains. Each of them is
full of interest, replete with instruction, the work of a master's
hand. In the first, Jonah himself is the central figure. His
conversion is its subject. At its commencement he is self-
willed and refractory. At its close he is submissive and obedi-
ent. The Flight, the Storm, the Imprisonment in the fish, the
Prayer, the Deliverance, are the several scenes in this Act. Its
beginning and end are marked by the words, "Now the word of
the Lord came unto Jonah, saying, Arise, go to Nineveh...but
Jonah rose up to flee unto Tarshish from the presence of the
Lord" (c. i. 1—3); "And the word of the Lord came unto Jonah
the second time, saying, Arise, go unto Nineveh...So Jonah arose
and went unto Nineveh, according to the word of the Lord"
(c. iii. 1—3). The second Act as we have called it concentrates
our attention on "that great city" Nineveh. Its repentance
and salvation are now the engrossing theme. In the simple

grandeur of its vast size, imagination being left to complete the picture, to fill in that great area with royal palaces and crowded marts and gardens and vineyards and parks and pleasances, the city stands before us. Scene follows upon scene in quick and lifelike succession. The solitary stranger enters Nineveh as "a voice crying," not in the wilderness but in the city, no word or deed of his within its precincts recorded but this, that as he went he said "Yet forty days, and Nineveh shall be over-thrown." The scene changes. "Lamentation and mourning and woe" are heard in every quarter of that vast city, "All joy is darkened, the mirth of the land is gone." Costly ap-parel is exchanged for sackcloth. Sumptuous fare gives place to fasting. Even the lower animals are included in the uni-versal sorrow and humiliation. Business and pleasure alike cease. Nineveh is one vast temple of penitence and prayer. Yet another and no less striking scene brings this act to a conclu-sion. Their prayer is heard, their repentance is accepted, their city is spared, the stream of their life purified and renewed returns to its accustomed course. The cloud that hung threat-eningly over their city is dispersed, and the sun shines forth upon it again. "And God saw their works, that they turned from their evil way, and God repented of the evil, that He had said that He would do unto them : and He did it not" (c. iii. 10). But this, however morally grand and impressive, is not the climax of the history. The teaching of the book of Jonah does not end here. There remains another Act in which the prophet himself is again the chief character. Jonah displeased at the result of his mission, irritated and complaining, weary of life, and praying that he may die; Jonah sojourning in the hut which he has built him on the hill-side without the walls of the city, watching thence with evil eye the fortunes of Nineveh ; Jonah exceeding glad of the shady plant which God had mercifully prepared to overshadow his booth and screen him from the heat, vexed and angry even unto death again when that welcome alleviation is withdrawn ; Jonah convinced and silenced by the divinely-drawn contrast between his own selfish sorrow for a plant, and God's large and liberal pity for the populous city of Nineveh—these are the scenes portrayed with the same brevity and vigour as before in this final Act or chapter of the work.

4. But the book of Jonah is complete as a whole as well as thus complete in its several parts. The three Acts make one drama, the three movements form one composition. For the true harmonising "idea," which while it gives unity to the whole adds force and lustre to the several parts, we are indebted to the teaching of the New Testament. It is by the light of the later revelation that we discern the meaning and unity of this portion of the earlier. Our Lord, as we have seen already, regards Jonah as a type of Himself. He teaches us to see in this book an historical parable, a prophecy in act. As Jonah was swallowed by the fish, so Christ was laid in the heart of the earth. As Jonah after three days was cast up alive and unharmed on dry ground, so Christ rose again the third day from the dead. As Jonah went forth from his living prison to preach to the Ninevites (the only instance of a Jewish Prophet sent to the heathen), so Christ after His resurrection went forth, not in His own person, but by the agency of His Church, to preach the Gospel in all the world. The typical teaching of the book may be summed up, as has been said, in the words of St Paul, "That Christ should suffer, and that He should be the first that should rise from the dead, and should shew light unto the people (of Israel), and to the Gentiles[1]." Thus the lesson of repentance and the rebuke of exclusiveness take a higher, because in fact a Christian form, while the claim of this book to a place in the canon of Old Testament prophecy is amply justified. The history of Jonah is a part of that great onward movement, which was before the Law and under the Law, which gained strength and volume as the fulness of the times drew near, but which could only find its consummation in the Incarnation and work of Him in whom all distinctions of country and race were to be for ever broken down, in Whose name repentance and remission of sins were to be preached among

---

[1] Matthew xii. 40, 41; Acts xxvi. 23.

all nations[1], in Whom all nations of the earth were to be blessed, Who was to be at once a light to lighten the Gentiles, and the glory of His people Israel.

CHAPTER IV.

ANALYSIS OF CONTENTS.

The book of Jonah may conveniently be divided into four sections, corresponding almost exactly with the four chapters in our English Bibles.

I. Jonah's disobedience and punishment, ch. i. 1—17.

Jonah, sent on a divine mission to Nineveh, refuses to go, and takes ship to flee to Tarshish, i. 1—3.

Overtaken by a storm sent by God to arrest him in his flight, he is, at his own request, cast into the sea by the sailors, after all their efforts to save the ship have proved unavailing. The sea then becomes calm, i. 4—16.

II. Jonah's prayer and deliverance, ch. i. 17—ii. 10.

Swallowed alive by a great fish, prepared by God for the purpose, Jonah remains in the belly of the fish three days and three nights, i. 17.

He offers a prayer of thanksgiving for the deliverance from death by drowning already accorded him, mingled with confident expectation of yet further rescue, ii. 1—9.

At the command of God the fish casts him up on dry land, ii. 10.

III. Jonah's preaching and its result, ch. iii.

Profiting by the chastisement he has undergone, Jonah promptly obeys a second command to go to Nineveh, iii. 1—3.

He delivers there his startling message, "Yet forty days, and Nineveh shall be overthrown," iii. 4.

The Ninevites believe God and repent, and the threatened judgment is averted, iii. 5—10.

IV. Jonah's displeasure and its rebuke, ch. iv.

This result of his mission displeases Jonah exceedingly, and he complains to God against it, iv. 1—4.

---

[1] Luke xxiv. 47.

Still hoping, as it would seem, that Nineveh may be overthrown, he constructs for himself a booth without the walls, and sits beneath its shade to watch the fate of the city, iv. 5.

God causes a shady plant to spring up quickly and cover his booth, so as to shelter him from the burning heat of the sun; but the comfort thus afforded him is speedily withdrawn by the sudden withering of the plant, iv. 6, 7.

His grief for the loss of the plant is made the occasion by God of rebuking his want of pity for Nineveh, and of justifying His own merciful compassion in sparing that great city with its teeming population and exceeding much cattle, iv. 8—11.

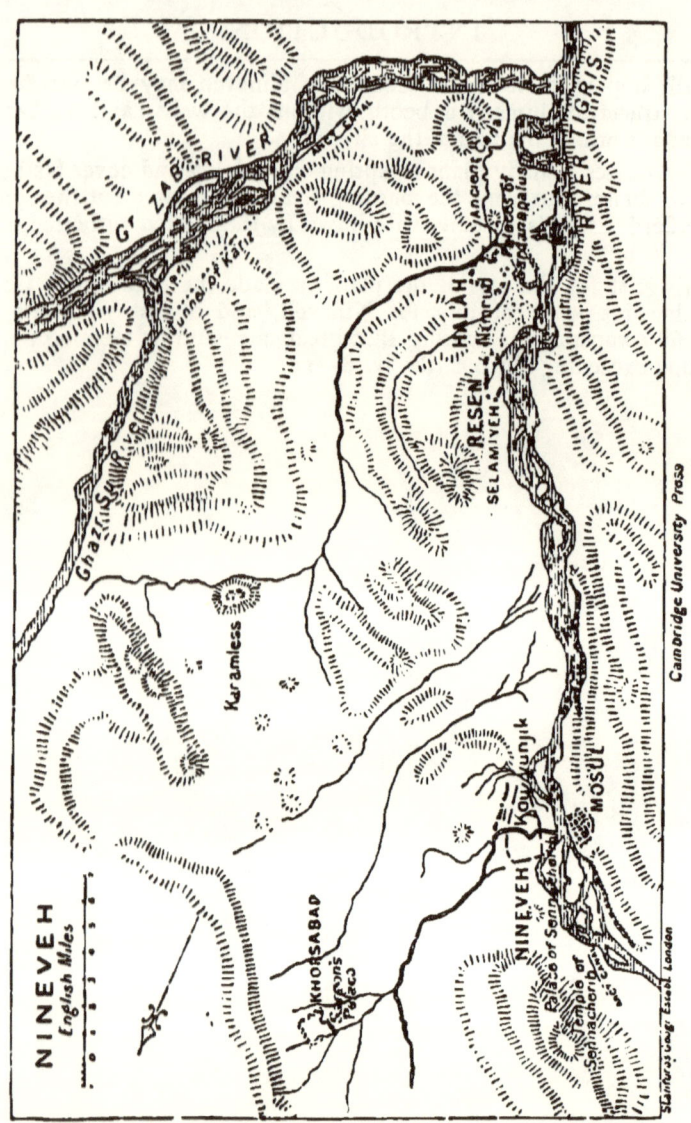

NINEVEH
English Miles

Karamless

KHORSABAD
Sargon's Palace

NINEVEH Kouyunjik
Palace of Sennacherib
Temple of Sennacherib

MOSUL

RIVER TIGRIS

Gr ZAB RIVER

HALAH
RESEN
SELAMIYEH
Nimrud
Ancient
Ruins of
Calah Kalakh

Ghazr Su

Wadi-ol-Kani

Stanford's Geog. Estab. London

Cambridge University Press

JONAH.

1—3. *Jonah's Disobedience.*

Now the word of the LORD came unto Jonah the son of 1
Amittai, saying, Arise, go to Nineveh, *that* great city, 2
and cry against it; for their wickedness is come up before me. But Jonah rose up to flee unto Tarshish from the 3
presence of the LORD, and went down *to* Joppa; and he

CH. I. 1—3. JONAH'S DISOBEDIENCE.

1. *Now the word*, &c.] Lit., "**And** the word," &c. There is no
reason to conclude from this that the Book of Jonah is only a fragment
of a larger work. Many books of the Old Testament begin with
"And." In some cases (e.g. Exodus, Leviticus, Numbers, 2 Samuel)
they do so, because the writer wishes to mark the fact that the book so
commencing is a continuation, a second or third volume so to speak, of
what he has written before. In other cases, as here and in Ezekiel i. 1,
the author begins his work with the words, "And it was," "And it
came to pass," because, though he may have written nothing before
himself, yet there is a reference *in his own mind* to the national records
that had gone before, and he consciously takes up the thread of past
history. See Maurer on Ezek. i. 1.

2. *Nineveh*] On the E. bank of the Tigris, the capital of the ancient
kingdom and empire of Assyria, and "the most magnificent of all the
capitals of the ancient world." The building of it is mentioned as early
as Gen. x. 11. In the time of Jonah it appears to have been at the
zenith of its glory.

that great city] See note on c. iii. 3, and Note B.

3. *Tarshish*] Probably Tartessus, an ancient mercantile city of the
Phœnicians, in the S. of Spain, of which the site is supposed to have
been "between the two arms by which the Guadalquivir flowed into the
sea." See Smith's *Bib. Dict.* Art. *Tarshish.* "God bid him go to
Nineveh, which lay North-East from his home, and he instantly set himself to flee to the then furthermost West."—Pusey.

from the presence of the Lord] This may mean from standing before
the Lord or being in His presence, as His servant or minister (Deut. x. 8,
1 Kings xvii. 1, Matthew xviii. 10, Luke i. 19. See Dr Pusey, *Commentary
on Jonah*, p. 247, note d.); i.e. he renounced his office of prophet rather

found a ship going *to* Tarshish: so he paid the fare thereof,
and went down into it, to go with them unto Tarshish from
the presence of the LORD.

than obey so unwelcome a command. It may, however, only refer to
that special presence of God in the Holy Land, which all Jews recognised.
Either view is compatible with a belief on the part of Jonah in the om-
nipresence of God (Ps. cxxxix.). It is said of Cain (Gen. iv. 16) that
he "went out from the presence of the Lord" (and the Heb. phrase
is the same as here), when he forfeited the favourable regard, together
possibly with some local manifestation of the presence of the Almighty.

The reason of Jonah's disobedience is given by himself, ch. iv. 2.
Knowing well the lovingkindness of God, he anticipated that He would
spare the Ninevites on their repentance, and he could not bring himself to be the messenger of mercy to heathen, much less to heathen who
(as the Assyrian inscriptions state) had already made war against his
own people, and who as he may have known were destined to be their
conquerors. See the statements of his probable contemporary, Hosea,
ix. 3, xi. 5.

Joppa] Now Jaffa, the well-known port of Palestine on the Mediterranean. It was 50 miles from Gath-hepher.

"Jaffa is one of the oldest cities in the world. It was given to
Dan (?), in the distribution of the land by Joshua, and it has been known
to history ever since. It owes its existence to the low ledge of rocks,
which extends into the sea from the extremity of the little cape on
which the city stands, and forms a small harbour. Insignificant as it is
and insecure, yet there being no other in all this coast, it was sufficient
to cause a city to spring up around it even in the earliest times, and to
sustain its life through numberless changes of dynasties, races and
religions, down to the present hour. It was in fact the only harbour of
any notoriety possessed by the Jews throughout the greater part of their
national existence. To it the timber for both the temples of Jerusalem
was brought from Lebanon; and no doubt a lucrative trade in cedar
and pine was always carried on through it with the nations who had
possession of the forests of Lebanon. Through it also nearly all the
foreign commerce of the Jews was conducted until the artificial port of
Cæsarea was built by Herod."

"The harbour, however, is very inconvenient and insecure. Vessels
of any considerable burden must lie out in the open roadstead—a very
uneasy berth at all times; and even a moderate wind will oblige them
to slip cable and run out to sea, or seek anchorage at Haifa, sixty miles
distant. The landing also is most inconvenient, and often extremely
dangerous. More boats upset and more lives are lost in the breakers at
the north end of the ledge of rocks that defend the inner habour,
than anywhere else on this coast. I have been in imminent danger
myself, with all my family in the boat, and never look without a shudder
at this treacherous port, with its noisy surf tumbling over the rocks, as
if on purpose to swallow up unfortunate boats."—Thomson, *Land and
Book*, pp. 514—516; see also Smith's *Bible Dict.* Art. *Joppa.*

4—16. *Jonah's Punishment. The Storm and its consequences.*

But the LORD sent out a great wind into the sea, and there 4 was a mighty tempest in the sea, so that the ship was like to be broken. Then the mariners were afraid, and cried every 5 man unto his god, and cast forth the wares that *were* in the

4—16. JONAH'S PUNISHMENT. THE STORM AND ITS CONSEQUENCES.

No sooner does Jonah decide upon his course of action and think himself now secure of its accomplishment, than God arrests him by the judgment of the storm.

4. *sent out*] Lit., as in margin, **cast forth**, indicating the suddenness and violence of the storm. The same word occurs and is rendered "cast forth" in A.V. in *vv.* 5, 12, 15.

Josephus speaks of a violent wind called "the black North wind," which he says sometimes visited the sea off the coast of Joppa. And we read of "a tempestuous wind called Euraquilo" in another part of the same sea, which rushing down the highlands of Crete suddenly caught the ship in which St Paul was sailing, and brought on a tempest scarcely less severe than that to which Jonah was exposed (Acts xxvii. 14). The modern name *Levanter* is a witness to the prevalence of such winds in those seas.

was like to be broken] Lit., **thought to be broken**, as in the margin. A vivid image or personification in keeping with the graphic style of this book. The same word "broken," i.e. "broken up," or "broken in pieces," is used of a ship that is wrecked in 1 Kings xxii. 48. Comp. Acts xxvii. 41.

5, 6. The conduct of the heathen mariners stands in striking and favourable contrast with that of the Jewish prophet. They call upon their gods and use every effort to save the ship. He, moody, miserable, and weary with mental conflict and bodily fatigue, is sunk in deep sleep, and has to be roused to consciousness and prayer by the reproaches of the heathen captain.

5. *the mariners*] The Hebrew word is formed from the word for *salt*, and denotes those occupied with the salt sea. So we sometimes speak of a sailor as a "salt."

See note on next verse, and for the whole description of their terror and their prayer comp. Ps. cvii. 23—30; Matt. viii. 23—27.

every man unto his god] They were probably Phoenicians, who had the carrying trade between Joppa and Tarshish. This would account for their multiplicity of gods. The crew, however, may have been composed of men of different nations. Comp.

> "All lost! to prayers, to prayers! All lost!"
> Shakespeare, *The Tempest*, Act I. Sc. v.

the wares] It is doubtful whether this includes the cargo. It may

ship into the sea, to lighten *it* of them. But Jonah was gone
down into the sides of the ship; and he lay, and was fast
6 asleep. So the shipmaster came to him, and said unto him,

only mean the furniture of the ship, moveables, spare tackling, etc.
In St Paul's shipwreck a similar course was taken (Acts xxvii. 19), but
the cargo was not thrown overboard till a later period (ver. 38). Jonah's
ship may have been, like St Paul's, a corn ship. The export of corn
from Joppa was very considerable. See 1 Kings v. 9; Ezek. xxvii. 17;
Acts xii. 20.

to lighten it of them] Rather, **to lighten** (the burden) **from upon
them** (the mariners), i. e. to make matters easier for them. Comp.
Exod. xviii. 22, where the same Hebrew phrase is rendered "it shall be
easier for thyself." *Unto them*, R.V.

the sides of the ship] The Hebrew word is not the same as that
rendered "ship" earlier in the verse. It occurs nowhere else in the
O. T., but the verb from which it is derived signifies to *'cover'* or *'board
over'* (1 Kings vii. 3, 7), so that it is probably used to denote that it
was a *decked* vessel in which Jonah sailed, and that he had, as we should
say, gone down below. The "sides of the ship" are what we should
call the bottom of the ship, the part in which the two sides meet. The
same expression is used of the innermost recess of a cave, the point of
meeting of the two sides (1 Sam. xxiv. 3). *Innermost parts*, R.V.

was fast asleep] Jonah had probably fallen asleep before the storm
commenced, and slumbered too deeply to be roused by it, or by the
commotion on board. Our Lord's sleep amidst the storm on the lake
(Mark iv. 38) furnishes at once a comparison and a contrast. Kalisch
quotes in illustration of the heavy sleep of sorrow the case of the
disciples in the Garden; "He found them sleeping for sorrow," Luke
xxii. 45; and the words of Sallust, "primo cura, dein, uti aegrum
animum solet, somnus cepit," *Bell. Jug.* c. 71.

6. *the shipmaster*] Lit., **the chief of the sailors**, i. e. the captain.
The word here for *sailors* (which is singular and used collectively) is not
the same word as that rendered *mariners* in *v.* 5. It is formed from the
Hebrew word for a rope, and means properly those who handle the
ropes. Both words occur again (and it is the only other place in the
O. T. where either of them is found) in the description of the maritime
greatness of Tyre in Ezekiel xxvii. The word used in this verse is
there rendered in *vv.* 8, 27, 29, *pilots*, and the mention of their wisdom
in *v.* 8 has been thought to justify this distinction. It should be
observed, however, that the contrast there is between mere *rowers* (for
so, and not *mariners*, the other word in that verse should be rendered)
who were hired from Sidon and Arvad, and *skilled sailors*, who were
the product of Tyre herself. The word rendered *mariners* in *v.* 5 of
this chapter and in Ezek. xxvii. 9, 27, 29, appears to be a more
general word, including all seafaring persons. The Hebrews, not
being a maritime nation, make but little use of nautical terms. We
have in addition to the words just mentioned the expressions, "ship-
men that had knowledge of the sea" (lit., "men of ships, knowing the

What meanest thou, O sleeper? arise, call upon thy God, if
so be that God will think upon us, that we perish not.

And they said every one to his fellow, Come, and let us 7
cast lots, that we may know for whose cause this evil *is* upon

sea"), 1 Kings ix. 27 (comp. 2 Chron. viii. 18); "They that go down
to the sea in ships," Psalm cvii. 23, or simply, "They that go down to
the sea," Isaiah xlii. 10.

What meanest thou, O sleeper?] Lit., **What (is there) to thee,
sleeping?** i.e. What reason hast thou for sleeping? The A.V. and R.V.
apparently take the participle "sleeping" as a vocative, "O sleeper?"
What meanest thou by sleeping! would perhaps be the best translation. It
is an exclamation of indignant surprise at the unreasonableness of Jonah's
conduct. The word for sleep here and in *v.* 5 means heavy or deep
sleep, such as Adam's (Gen. ii. 21), or Sisera's (Judg. iv. 21). LXX. τί
σὺ ῥέγχεις;

God] This abstract use of the word (lit., **"the God"**) immediately
after "*thy* God" in this verse, and the mention in *v.* 6 that the
mariners "cried every man unto *his* god," is remarkable. It would
seem to imply, as Calvin argues, that behind and above the many gods
whom the heathen invented for themselves, they retained the idea,
vague perhaps and indistinct for the most part, but starting into prominence in times of danger and distress such as this, of one supreme God
by whose providence the world is governed, and in whose hand are the
life and safety of all men.

will think upon us] Some would render, "will brighten, or shine
upon us," i.e. will be propitious or favourable to us; but there seems
no reason to depart from the A.V., which the R.V. retains.

7. Finding their prayers as unavailing as their efforts, the sailors
conclude that the storm is sent upon them by the gods as a judgment
for some crime committed by one of their number; and they proceed
to cast lots to discover who the culprit is. Instances of a similar belief
on the part of the heathen have been adduced from classical authors
(see Rosenmüller and Maurer *in loc.*). A story is told by Cicero (*de
Nat. Deor.* III. 37) of Diagoras, how that when he was on a voyage,
and the sailors, terrified by a storm which had befallen them, charged
him with being the cause of it, he pointed to other vessels in the same
plight with themselves, and asked them whether they thought that they
too carried Diagoras. Horace, in a well-known passage, affirms that he
would not suffer a man, who had provoked the anger of the gods, to
put to sea in the same boat with him, because the innocent in such
cases were not unfrequently involved in a common punishment with the
guilty (Hor. *Od.* lib. III. c. 2. 26—30). The truth, which underlay this
wide spread conviction, is taught us in its pure form in such histories as
those of Achan (Josh. vii.) and Jonathan (1 Sam. xiv. 36—46).

for whose cause] Lit., **on account of (that) which (refers) to whom**,
i.e. on whose account. The same expression occurs in *v.* 12 ("*for my
sake*"), and, though in the Hebrew in an uncontracted form, in *v.* 8

8 us. So they cast lots, and the lot fell upon Jonah. Then said they unto him, Tell us, we pray thee, for whose cause this evil *is* upon us; What *is* thine occupation? and whence comest thou? what *is* thy country? and of what people *art* 9 thou? And he said unto them, I *am* a Hebrew; and I fear the LORD, the God of heaven, which hath made the sea and

the lot fell upon Jonah] An illustration of Prov. xvi. 33; comp. Josh. vii. 18; 1 Sam. xiv. 42. It is worthy of note that the use of the lot, though frequently mentioned and sanctioned in the O.T., and employed even after the Ascension in the choice of an Apostle to fill the place of Judas, never occurs in the Bible after the day of Pentecost. It would seem to have been superseded and rendered needless by the gift which conferred "a right judgment in all things."

8. *for whose cause*] The lot has detected Jonah, but they will not condemn him unheard. They will give him an opportunity of clearing himself, or like Achan (Josh. vii. 19), of making confession with his own lips. The judicial fairness and calmness of these heathen men, their abstinence from anger and reproach for the wrong done them, their sense of the sanctity of human life, their fear of punishing the innocent, are very strikingly brought out in the whole of this exciting scene.

"Even in their supreme danger the mariners were anxious not only to avoid all violence, but all haste. While the fury of the waves and the tempest constantly increased, and every instant was precious to those who prized their lives, they patiently instituted an investigation with almost judicial calmness. Though fully trusting to the reality of the decision by lot, they were resolved neither to execute the judgment without the offender's confession, nor to execute it in an arbitrary manner." Kalisch, who quotes the words of Philo: "One might see in the scene a terrible tribunal: for the ship was the court of justice, the judges were the sailors, the executioners were the winds, the prisoner at the bar was the prophet, the house of correction and prison of safe keeping was the whale, and the accuser was the angry sea."

What is thine occupation, &c.] This crowding together of questions in their excitement is very true to nature. It has been compared with the well-known passage in Virgil, *Æn.* VIII. 112—114.

9. The emergency recalls Jonah to his true self. All the better part of his character now comes out. His conduct throughout the remainder of the chapter is dignified and manly, worthy of a servant and prophet of Jehovah.

a Hebrew] This is the name by which the Jews were known to *foreigners* (comp. the use of it by Juvenal and other classical writers). It is quite in keeping with Biblical usage that Jonah employs it in describing himself to the heathen sailors. Had he been addressing one of his own countrymen, he would have spoken of himself as an *Israelite.*

I fear the Lord] Rather, **I fear Jehovah.** They knew already

the dry *land.* Then were the men exceedingly afraid, and 10
said unto him, Why hast thou done this? For the men knew
that he fled from the presence of the LORD, because he had
told them. Then said they unto him, What shall we do unto 11
thee, that the sea may be calm unto us? for the sea wrought,
and was tempestuous. And he said unto them, Take me up, 12
and cast me forth into the sea; so shall the sea be calm unto

(*v.* 10) that he was a worshipper of Jehovah, and that he had offended
Him, and was fleeing from His presence. But hitherto they had only
looked upon Jehovah as *a* god, one of many, with whom they had no
concern. Comp. Pharaoh's contemptuous question, "Who is Jehovah,
that I should obey his voice, to let Israel go? I know not Jehovah,
neither will I let Israel go." Ex. v. 2. Now, however, when Jonah
added that Jehovah was the God of heaven, who had made the sea and
the dry land, while the tempest raged still to confirm his words, "The
men were exceedingly afraid."

10. *Why hast thou done this?*] Rather, **What is this that thou
hast done?** A question not of enquiry, but of amazement and reproach. Comp. Gen. iv. 10.

11. *What shall we do unto thee*] No doubt in their thus appealing
to Jonah to tell them what was to be done, instead of at once ridding
themselves of him as the acknowledged cause of their calamity, we may
recognise their reverence for Jehovah, and in a measure also for His
servant. At the same time it was only natural and reasonable that,
having learned of him the cause, they should seek to know from him
the cure of their trouble. "Since you are a worshipper of the most High
and Almighty God, you ought to know how the anger of your God can
be appeased."—Rosenm.

may be calm unto us] Lit., **may be quiet from upon us,** *i. e.* from
pressing upon us and being hostile to us. The word used for being
quiet or silent in this and the next verse only occurs beside in Ps. cvii.
30, of quiet after a storm at sea, and in Prov. xxvi. 20, of the ceasing
of strife.

wrought, and was tempestuous] Lit., **was going and being tossed,**
i. e. according to the Hebrew idiom, became increasingly tempestuous.
So in Gen. viii. 3, "the waters returned from off the earth continually,"
is literally, "returned to go and to return," i.e. returned increasingly, or
more and more. *Grew more and more tempestuous,* R.V.

12. *cast me forth into the sea*] "The question is raised whether
Jonah ought of his own accord to have offered himself to death; for his
doing so seems to be a sign of despair. He might, indeed, have sur-
rendered himself to their will, but here he, as it were, incites them to
the deed. *Cast me into the sea,* he says, for in no other way will you
appease God, than by punishing me. He seems like a man in despair
when he thus goes at his own instance to death. But without doubt
Jonah recognised that he was divinely summoned to punishment. It is
uncertain whether he then conceived a hope of preservation, whether,

you: for I know that for my sake this great tempest *is* upon
13 you.   Nevertheless the men rowed hard to bring *it* to the
land; but they could not: for the sea wrought, and was
14 tempestuous against them.   Wherefore they cried unto the
LORD, and said, We beseech thee, O LORD, we beseech thee,
let us not perish for this man's life, and lay not upon us
innocent blood: for thou, O LORD, hast done as it pleased

that is, with a present confidence, he rested on the grace of God; but,
however that be, one may gather that he goes forth to death because he
perceives and is assuredly persuaded that he is in a manner summoned
by the clear voice of God.   And so there is no doubt that he patiently
undergoes the judgment which the Lord has brought against him."—
Calvin.

   13. *rowed hard*] Lit., **digged.**   The word is used for digging or
breaking through a wall, Job xxiv. 16; Ezek. xii. 5, 7.   The figurative
use of it does not occur again in the O. T., where, as has been before
observed, the references to maritime affairs are very few, but the figure
itself is common in other languages.   Rosenm. compares the phrases
"infindere sulcos," "arare aquas," "scindere freta." Virg. *Æn.* v. 142,
Ovid, *Trist.* III. *Eleg.* XII. 36, *Metamorph.* XI. 463.   They used their
utmost endeavours to bring her to land again, but in vain, for the tempest, so far from abating, only raged more furiously.

   14—16.   The openness of these heathens to religious impressions;
the readiness with which they acknowledged Jehovah (hitherto to them
an unknown God), and addressed no longer to their own gods (*v.* 5),
but to Him their most earnest and humble prayers; their submission to
His will (*v.* 14), and the worship which they subsequently paid and
promised Him (*v.* 15), are all brought out in bold relief, and in strong
and (in pursuance of the object of this Book) intended contrast with
the conduct of His own people Israel in turning from Him to idols.
These heathens, too, reverence and would fain save from death a prophet .
of Jehovah who has come to them unbidden, and has well-nigh compassed their destruction; Jerusalem "killed the prophets and stoned
them that were sent unto her" for her salvation.   They shew the
utmost tenderness for a single life; Jonah, the prophet of the Lord, is
worse than regardless of "more than sixscore thousand" human souls.

   14. *for this man's life*] i.e. for having taken it away.   Lit., **in** the
life of this man, according to a well-known use of this Heb. preposition in the sense of 'in the place of,' 'in exchange for.'   So Gen.
xxix. 18, "I will serve thee for (lit. 'in,' in exchange for) Rachel;"
and Deut. xix. 21, "life for (in) life," &c.

   lay not upon us innocent blood] i.e. the guilt of having shed innocent
blood.   Comp. Deut xxi. 8.

   for thou, O Lord, &c.] The death of this man is no doing of ours.
We are only carrying out Thy declared will.   Hold us not, therefore,
responsible for it.   "That Jonah betook himself to this ship of ours,

thee. So they took up Jonah, and cast him forth into the 15
sea: and the· sea ceased from her raging. Then the men 16
feared the LORD exceedingly, and offered a sacrifice unto
the LORD, and made vows.

i. 17—ii. 10. *Jonah's Prayer and Deliverance.*

Now the LORD had prepared a great fish to swallow up 17

that the tempest was raised, that Jonah was taken by lot, that he passed
this sentence upon himself, all this comes of Thy will."—Rosenm.

15. *they took up*] With respect and reluctance, with no struggle on
his part, or violence on theirs.

her raging] Lit., **her anger.** "Maris ira," Ovid. *Met.* I. 330,
"iratum mare," Hor. *Epod.* II. 5, 6, are quoted by the commentators.

16. *feared the Lord exceedingly*] They had feared exceedingly before
(*v.* 10, where the Heb. expression is the same as here), but their fear
then was vague and indefinite, now it recognised as its object Jehovah,
the God of Jonah.

offered a sacrifice] It would certainly seem to be implied, that immediately on the ceasing of the storm the sailors offered a sacrifice to
Jonah's God, in acknowledgment of what He had already done, and at
the same time vowed that they would present to Him other gifts and
offerings when He should have brought them safe to land. We know
but little of the ships of the ancients, but some of them were of considerable size, and there is no difficulty in supposing that there may
have been one or more live animals suitable for sacrifice on board
Jonah's ship.

I. 17—II. 10. JONAH'S PRAYER AND DELIVERANCE.

Cast into the sea at his own request by the sailors, Jonah is swallowed
alive by a large fish, and remains uninjured inside it for three days and
three nights, i. 17. While there, he offers a prayer of thanksgiving to
Almighty God (ii. 1—9), at whose command the fish, at the end of the
three days and three nights, vomits up Jonah on the dry land, ii. 10.

17 *had prepared*] Rather: **assigned,** or **appointed.** (LXX. προσέ-
ταξε.) The same word and tense are used of the gourd, the worm, and
the East wind, ch. iv. 6, 7, 8. They do not necessarily imply any
previous or special *preparation*, much less the *creation* of these various
agents for the purpose to which they were put; but merely that they
were appointed to it by Him, whom "all things serve." He sent the
fish there to do His bidding. The word is rendered "appointed" in
Job vii. 3, Dan. i. 5, 10; and "set" in Dan. i. 11.

"By God's immediate direction it was so arranged that the very
moment when Jonah was thrown into the waves, the 'great fish' was
on the spot to receive him; God charged the animal to perform this
function, as He afterwards 'spoke to' it (*v.* 10), or commanded it, to
vomit out the prophet on the dry land."—Kalisch.

a great fish] Probably a shark. See note A.

Jonah. And Jonah was in the belly of the fish three days
2 and three nights. Then Jonah prayed unto the LORD his
2 God out of the fish's belly, and said,

three days and three nights] At this point the transaction becomes
clearly miraculous. The swallowing of Jonah by the fish may have
been in the course of the ordinary working of divine Providence. His
preservation within it for so long a time plainly belongs to that other
working of Almighty God which, though it be no less after the counsel
of that Will (Ephes. i. 11) which is the highest and only Law, appears
to us to be extraordinary, and which we therefore call *miraculous*.

A comparison of 1 Cor. xv. 4 with Matt. xii. 40 shows that the period
of Jonah's incarceration in the fish was divinely ordered to be a type of
our Lord's being "three days and three nights in the heart of the
earth." This is the only passage in the O. T., if we except Hosea
vi. 2, in which there is any prophetical intimation of the length of time
between our Lord's burial and resurrection.

CH. II.—1. *Then Jonah prayed*] What follows, *vv.* 2—9, is rather
a thanksgiving than a prayer. The same, however, may be said of
Hannah's utterance (1 Sam. ii. 1—10), which is introduced by the same
word ("Hannah *prayed*"). Comp. Acts xvi. 25, where Alford renders
"praying, sung praises," or "in their prayers were singing praises,"
and remarks that "the distinction of modern times between prayer and
praise arising from our attention being directed to the *shape* rather than
to the essence of devotion, was unknown in these days: see Col. iv. 2."
It has, indeed, been held (Maurer) that Jonah does pray here, and that
the past tenses (*v.* 2, &c.) are in reality present and only in form past,
because they are literal quotations from some of the Psalms. It is
simpler, however, to suppose, with the great majority of commentators,
that Jonah had prayed to God in the prospect and the act of being cast
into the sea, while he was being buffeted by the waves and sinking into
the depths, and in the agony of being swallowed by the fish. During
all this time, whether his lips spoke or not, his mind was fixed in that
intent Godward attitude and posture which is the truest prayer. Now,
however, when he finds himself alive and unharmed in that strange
abode, he prays no longer, but offers thanksgivings for the measure of
deliverance already granted him in answer to those former prayers,
mingled with joyful anticipations of the yet further deliverance which
the last verse of the chapter records. It seems probable that Jonah's
prayer was offered at the end of the three days and nights, and was
followed immediately by his release. How the three days and nights
were spent by him, whether in unconsciousness, as some have thought,
or in godly sorrow and repentance, like Saul at Damascus, as others
have held, we have no means of knowing.

his God] When Jonah flees in disobedience it is "from the presence
of Jehovah;" when he prays in penitence, it is to "Jehovah *his God*."
Comp. "O Lord my God," *v.* 6, and "*my* God," Psalm xxii. 1.

2. *and said*] The prayer which follows falls naturally into three
parts or divisions. In each of these the two elements of danger and

I cried by reason of mine affliction unto the LORD, and
he heard me;

deliverance, of need and help, appear. But they enter into them in
very different proportions. Faith grows, and the prospect brightens at
each fresh stage of the hymn. The first rises to prayer, the second to
confidence, the third to thankfulness and praise.

I. *vv.* 2—4.
   (1) Introduction, containing the general subject of the hymn : I
       cried and was heard, I was in trouble and was delivered.
       v. 2.
   (2) Description of the danger and distress. *v.* 3.
   (3) Faith triumphing over despondency and prompting to prayer.
       v. 4.

II. *vv.* 5, 6.
   (1) More vivid description of the danger and distress. *vv.* 5, 6*a*.
   (2) Deliverance not only prayed for, but possessed. *v.* 6*b*.

III. *vv.* 7—9.
   (1) Prayer, offered in danger and distress, has been heard. *v.* 7.
   (2) God, no longer forsaken, but sought and recognised as the
       fountain of mercy, has granted deliverance which shall be
       acknowledged with sacrifices of thanksgiving and vows
       joyfully paid. *vv.* 8, 9*a*.
   (3) All salvation, as this typical instance shows, is of God. *v.* 9*b*.

The prayer is remarkable for its many resemblances in thought and
expression to passages in the Book of Psalms. The words of the
Psalter, however, are not exactly and literally quoted, but its ideas
and phrases are freely wrought into the prayer, as if drawn from the
well-stored memory of a pious Israelite, familiar with its contents, and
naturally giving vent to his feelings in the cherished forms, which were
now instinct for him with new life and meaning. The manner in which
our English literature (not only sacred, but secular and even profane
and infidel) abounds in Scripture imagery and phraseology may help us
to understand how coincidences of this kind may have arisen, without
any deliberate intention on the part of a later writer to copy from an
earlier, or even any direct consciousness that he was doing so.

by reason of mine affliction]   Rather, as in A.V. and R.V. margin,
out of mine affliction, i.e. out of the midst of it, while it still compassed
me about. The time referred to is when he was in the sea.

The first half of this verse is identical in the Heb. words, though not in
their order, with Ps. cxx. 1, except that in the Psalm we have "in,"
instead of "from" or "out of" mine affliction, and a lengthened form
of the word for affliction is used. The coincidence cannot, however, be
properly said to affect the date of the Book of Jonah. The Psalm, it is

Out of the belly of hell cried I, *and* thou heardest my
voice.

3 For thou hadst cast me *into* the deep, in the midst of
the seas:
And the floods compassed me about:
All thy billows and thy waves passed over me.

4 Then I said, I am cast out of thy sight;

---

ture, belongs to a collection which "in its present form must have been
made after the return from Babylon" but it by no means follows that
no ode of the collection had been composed before that time. Besides,
the whole sentence is, both in language and idea, too commonplace, so
to speak, to be safely insisted upon as a quotation at all. Two quite
independent writers may easily have lighted on it. And moreover, if
quoted at all it may owe its origin no less probably to Psalm xvii.,
between which and the prayer of Jonah the resemblance, though less
exact in this particular verse, is as a whole more close and striking.
Comp. Ps. xviii. 6, 1st clause.

of hell] **The unseen world**, the place of the dead amongst whom,
when cast into the sea, he seemed already to be numbered. Comp. Ps.
xviii. 5, "the sorrows of hell (or rather "the bonds of the unseen
world") compassed me about."

3. *hadst cast*] There is no proper tense in the Heb. language.
There is no need, however, here to depart from the more literal rendering *castedst* or *didst cast*, R.V. See note on v. 1.

the deep] The same word is used (in the plur.) literally of Pharaoh
and his host, Ex. xv. 5, "They sank into the bottom," and metaphorically, Micah vii. 19.

the floods] Lit. **the river**. Used of the *current* or *flowing* of the
sea. "And the flowing of the sea surrounds me." Gesenius: 'das
strömen.' The same word occurs in the same sense, Ps. xxiv. 2.

All thy billows, &c.] Lit. "all **Thy breakers and Thy long rolling
waves**." Comp. "Quanti montes volvuntur aquarum." Ovid. *Trist.*
I. ii. 19. The whole clause occurs again in Ps. xlii. 7, though there it
is used metaphorically and here literally: or rather, to the metaphorical
sense is here superadded the literal. For by calling them "Thy"
breakers and waves, Jonah shews that to him, as to the Psalmist, the
sense of God's punishment and displeasure was the soul of his affliction.

4. *Then I said, &c.*] The first clause of this verse may, perhaps,
be a reminiscence of the first clause of Ps. xxxi. 22 (Heb. 23), though
there the words "in my haste" are added, and a different verb ("cut
off" instead of "cast out") is used. "Jonah substitutes the stronger
word. *I am cast forth*, driven forth, expelled, like the *mire and dirt*
(Is. lvii. 20) which the waves drive along, or like the waves themselves
in their restless motion (id., or the heathen (the word is the same)
whom God had driven out before Israel (Ex. xxxiv. 11), or as Adam
from Paradise. (Gen. iii. 24)."—Pusey.

Yet I will look again toward thy holy temple.
The waters compassed me about, *even* to the soul: 5
The depth closed me round about,
The weeds *were* wrapt about my head.
I went down to the bottoms of the mountains;   6
The earth *with* her bars *was* about me for ever:

thy holy temple] Not the heavenly temple or dwelling-place of God, but the literal temple. This is not, however, an expression of Jonah's confident belief that, outcast as he now seemed to be, he would certainly be delivered, and visit again, and behold once more with his bodily eyes the temple on Mount Sion. It is the then present thought and resolution with which, when he said "I am cast out of Thy sight," he corrected and overcame his unbelieving despondency. "One thing is left me still, one resource is still open to me, I will still pray, I will look (mentally) yet again towards Thy holy temple." The phrase "to look towards the temple," denoting prayer, has its origin in the prayer of Solomon at the dedication of the Temple. See 1 Kings viii. 29, 30, 48, and comp. Dan. vi. 10. The fact that Jonah was a prophet of the Northern Kingdom is no valid objection to this view. The Temple on Mount Sion was *the only centre* of the true worship of Jehovah, and was recognised as such by all faithful Israelites. But it would be enough to say with Calvin, "He had been circumcised, he had been a worshipper of God from his youth, he had been educated in the Law, he had been a constant participator in the sacrifices: under the name of the Temple he briefly comprehends all these things."

5. *compassed me about*] It would be better, perhaps, to render **surrounded me**, in order to show that this is a different word from that in *v.* 3, and then in the second clause of this verse, where the word is the same as in *v.* 3, to render **compassed me about**, instead of *closed me round about.*

to the soul] i.e. so as to endanger my soul, or life. Comp. Ps. lxix. 1 (where similar language is used figuratively) and Jer. iv. 10.

the weeds] The Heb. word is *sûph*, which so often occurs in the name Red Sea (lit., sea of *sûph*). "The *sûph* of the sea, it seems quite certain, is *a seaweed resembling wool*. Such sea-weed is thrown up abundantly on the shores of the Red Sea."—Smith's *Bible Dict.*, Art. *Red Sea.*

6. *bottoms*] Lit., as in margin, "**cuttings off**," the mountains being poetically conceived of as stretching away their roots or ridges to the lowest depths of the sea, and there ending or being cut off.

her bars] Lit., (**as for**) **the earth, her bars**, &c. The idea is that the gates of the earth were not only closed, but barred and made fast upon him, shutting him into the unseen world. The same word is used of Samson carrying away the gates of Gaza, "bar and all," i.e. probably a wooden beam used to hold fast the gates when they were closed. Judg. xvi. 3. Comp. "Let not the pit shut her mouth upon me," Ps. lxix. 15.

Yet hast thou brought up my life from corruption, O
LORD my God.

7 When my soul fainted within me I remembered the
LORD:
And my prayer came in unto thee, into thine holy
temple.

8 They that observe lying vanities forsake their own
mercy.

from corruption] Rather, **from the pit.** R. V.

7. *fainted*] Lit., **covered itself**; with reference to the film and
darkness that comes over eye and mind in fainting and exhaustion.
Comp. Pss. cxlii. 3, cvii. 5, where the same Heb. word occurs.

thine holy temple] at Jerusalem, as in *v.* 4.

8. *observe lying vanities*] Comp. Ps. xxxi. 6, where the same Heb.
word is rendered "regard." By "lying vanities" we are to understand "all inventions with which men deceive themselves" (Calvin),
all false, and therefore vain and disappointing objects of trust and confidence. Idols and false gods are no doubt included, but the sentiment
is conceived and expressed in the most general form, and therefore
embraces Jonah's own case. He had observed the lying vanity, the
deceitful promise of his own will and his own way, as opposed to God;
and not only had he found that God was stronger than he, but he had
been brought to see and confess that in such a course he had been his
own enemy.

forsake their own mercy] Rather, **their mercy.** Some (as Kalisch,
for example) would render, "they forget their kindness," i.e. "they
quickly and heedlessly forget the mercies they have enjoyed; the word
forsake being taken in the sense of *deserting*, or *dismissing*, viz. from
their thoughts," and "*their* mercies," as analogous to the phrase, *the
sure mercies of David* (Isai. lv. 3), "the benefits conferred upon or
enjoyed by David." But, apart from the meaning thus arbitrarily given
to the word "forsake," the sentiment attributed to the writer is unsatisfactory and untrue. "The suppliant declares," writes Kalisch, "I was
in distress, I prayed and was saved ; and now, unlike the idolaters who
gracelessly forget the bounties they have received, I shall evince my
gratitude to Jehovah by the voice of praise and by sacred gifts." But
it is not true that the idolaters in this sense "forget the benefits they
have received," as ch. i. 16 shows, and as the heathen temples filled
with votive offerings in acknowledgment of deliverance abundantly
testify.

By "their mercy" we are to understand God, who is the only source
of mercy and loving-kindness to all His creatures. The sentiment is
similar to that which is figuratively expressed by the prophet Jeremiah :
"They have forsaken Me, the fountain of living waters, and hewed
them out cisterns, broken cisterns, that can hold no water." (ii. 13.)
So God is called, "my mercy," Ps. cxliv. 2 (*margin*), the same word
being used as here.

But I will sacrifice unto thee with the voice of thanks- 9
giving;
I will pay *that* that I have vowed.
Salvation *is* of the LORD.
And the LORD spake unto the fish, and it vomited out 10
Jonah upon the dry *land*.

1—10. *Jonah's Preaching and its result.*

And the word of the LORD came unto Jonah the second 3
time, saying, Arise, go unto Nineveh, *that* great city, and 2
preach unto it the preaching that I bid thee. So Jonah 3
arose, and went unto Nineveh, according to the word of the

9. *But I*] in contrast to my former self, and to the whole body of those of whom I then was one, will humbly claim and gratefully acknowledge my share in "my Mercy." "I will sacrifice unto Thee," &c.

Salvation is of the Lord] Comp. Ps. iii. 8, Rev. vii. 10. This is at once confession and praise, a Creed and a *Te Deum*. It is the sum of his canticle, the outcome of all he has passed through. Deliverance in its fullest sense is already his in faith and confident anticipation. But God alone is the Author of it, and to Him alone shall the praise for it be ascribed. This point reached, Jonah's punishment has done its work, his discipline is at an end.

CH. III. 1—10. JONAH'S PREACHING AND ITS RESULT.

Sent a second time by God on a mission to Nineveh, Jonah promptly obeys, *vv.* 1—3*a*. He enters into Nineveh and delivers his message, *vv.* 3*b*—4. The Ninevites believe God and repent, *vv.* 5—9; and are spared, *v.* 10.

1—4. JONAH'S PREACHING.

1. *the second time*] Like St Peter (John xxi. 15—17), Jonah is not only forgiven, but restored to his office, and receives anew his commission.

2. *that great city*] Calvin explains this repeated mention of the greatness of Nineveh (comp. i. 2), as intended to prepare Jonah for the magnitude of the task before him, lest when he came face to face with it he should be appalled and draw back. But perhaps the true key is to be found in iv. 11, where the same expression "the great city" occurs as an argument for God's compassion. It is on no mean errand of mercy, not to save a few only from destruction, that I bid you go.

preach unto it the preaching] Lit., **cry to it the crying.** The word is rendered *cry*, i. 2.

3. *arose, and went*] Before, he *arose and fled*. He is still the same man. There is still the same energy and decision of character. But he is now "as ready to obey as before to disobey."

LORD. Now Nineveh was an exceeding great city of three

was] It has been asserted that the use of the past tense here, "according to all sound rules of interpretation, must be understood to imply that, in the author's time, Nineveh existed no longer," (Kalisch). Nothing, however, can safely be determined from the use of a tense in such cases. The clause "Now Nineveh was an exceeding great city," &c., is evidently a part of the narrative, and prepares the way for verse 4. It simply states what Nineveh was, and what Jonah found and saw it to be, when he visited it. It is not a historical note, like that which is introduced with reference to the building of Hebron, Numbers xiii. 22. St John writes (v. 2) "Now there *is* at Jerusalem by the sheep-gate a pool." It might be argued (as it has been) that because he uses the present tense, Jerusalem must have still been standing when he wrote his Gospel. Yet it might with equal force be concluded (and it is a proof of the unsatisfactory nature of this sort of criticism) that because he says that Bethany *was* nigh unto Jerusalem (xi. 18), that "Jesus went forth with His disciples over the brook Kedron, where *was* a garden" (xviii. 1), and that "in the place where He was crucified there *was* a garden" (xix. 41), the city and its environs were already laid waste when he wrote.

exceeding great] Lit., **great to God**. The expressions of this kind which occur in the Bible may be divided into two classes. They all alike spring out of the devout habit of the Hebrew mind, which recognises God in everything, and sees Him specially in whatever is best and greatest upon earth. But this habit of mind finds expression in two somewhat different ways. Sometimes, at the contemplation of what is more than ordinarily grand or beautiful, the pious mind rises at once to God, and recognises Him in His works. A thing so great, so fair, must be the work of His hands. "By the greatness and beauty of the creatures proportionably the Maker of them is seen."

"Who made you glorious as the gates of Heaven
Beneath the keen full moon?.........
God! let the torrents, like a shout of nations,
Answer! and let the ice-plains echo, God!"

Hence such expressions as "mountains of God," Ps. xxxvi. 6; "cedars of God," Ps. lxxx. 10; "trees of Jehovah," Ps. civ. 16; the explanation being added in the last of these instances (comp. Num. xxiv. 6), "which He hath planted." The other class of expressions are those in which the excellence of the object contemplated appears to suggest to the mind that it will bear the scrutiny of God's judgment, that even before Him, or as referred to Him, it is what the writer asserts it to be. To this class the expression here belongs. "Nineveh was a city, great, not only to man's thinking, but to God's." (Comp. ch. iv. 11.) In like manner we have, "a mighty hunter before the Lord," Gen. x. 9; "fair to God," Acts vii. 20.

of three days' journey] The most probable and most generally received opinion is that these words refer to the *circuit* of Nineveh, and that the

days' journey. And Jonah began to enter into the city a ₄

writer intends by them to say that the city was so large, that it would
take a man, walking at the usual pace, three days to go round it. This
would give about 60 miles for its circumference. See note B.

4. *And Jonah began to enter into the city*] Calvin well brings out
the moral grandeur of the scene which this verse so simply and briefly
describes; the promptitude of Jonah's action, in entering without delay
or hesitation or enquiry, immediately, as it would seem, upon his
reaching the city, upon his difficult and dangerous task; his boldness,
as a helpless and unprotected stranger, in standing in the heart of "the
bloody city," and denouncing destruction upon it. It was, indeed, to
"beard the lion in his den" to adventure himself on such an errand
into "the dwelling of the lions and the feeding place of the young
lions, where the lion, even the old lion, walked, and the lion's whelp,
and none made them afraid." (Nahum ii. 11.)

a day's journey] "He began to perambulate the city, going hither
and thither, as far as was possible, in the first day." (Maurer.) And
as he went he cried. In him was personified the description of the
wise King of Israel:

> "Wisdom crieth without;
> She uttereth her voice in the streets:
> She crieth in the chief place of concourse,
> in the openings of the gates:
> In the city she uttereth her words,
> Saying,
> ....
> Turn ye at my reproof."
>   Proverbs i. 20—23.

Some have supposed that, as a day's journey would suffice to traverse
from one side to the other a city, of which the dimensions were such
as have been assigned (v. 3) to Nineveh, and as, moreover, Jonah is
found afterwards (iv. 5) on the east side of Nineveh (i. e. the opposite
side to that on which he would have entered it in coming from Palestine), we are intended here to understand that he walked quite through
the city in a single day, uttering continually as he went "his one deep
cry of woe." The other view, however, is more natural, and it en-
hances the idea of the impressibility of the Ninevites, and their readiness
to believe and repent, which it is evidently the design of the inspired
writer to convey, if we suppose that while the preacher himself was seen
and heard in only a portion of the vast city, his message was taken up
and repeated, and sped and bore fruit rapidly in every direction, till
tidings of what was happening came to the king himself (v. 6), and in
obedience to the yet distant and unseen prophet, he issued the edict
which laid the whole of Nineveh, man and beast, abashed and humbled
before the threatened blow.

day's journey, and he cried, and said, Yet forty days, and
Nineveh *shall be* overthrown.

Yet forty days] "He threatens the overthrow of the city uncon-
ditionally. From the event, however, it is clear that the threat was to
be understood with this condition, 'unless ye shall (in the mean time)
have amended your life and conduct.' Comp. Jer. xviii. 7, 8."—
(Rosenm.) God's threatenings are always implied promises.

overthrown] The word is the same as that used of the destruction of
Sodom and Gomorrah, both in the history of that event (Gen. xix. 25,
29), and in subsequent reference to it (Deut. xxix. 23 [Heb. 22]). Not
necessarily by the same means, (comp. "overthrown by strangers,"
Isai. i. 7,) but as complete and signal shall the overthrow be. The use
of the participle, lit., **Yet forty days and Nineveh overthrown,** is
very forcible. To the prophet's eye, overlooking the short interval of
forty days, Nineveh appears not a great city with walls and towers and
palaces, and busy marts and crowded thoroughfares, but one vast mass
of ruins.

It may be asked whether the whole of Jonah's preaching to the
Ninevites consisted of this one sentence incessantly repeated. The
sacred text, taken simply as it stands, seems to imply that it did. We
have indeed here "the spectacle of an unknown Hebrew, in a prophet's austere and homely attire, passing through the splendid streets of
the proudest town of the Eastern world;" but not (except so far as
imagination completes the picture) of his "uttering words of rebuke
and menace, bidding the people not only to make restitution of their
unlawfully acquired property, but to give up their ancestral deities for
the one God of Israel." (Kalisch.) To an oriental mind (and Almighty
God is wont to adapt His means to those whom they are to reach) the
simple, oft-repeated announcement might be more startling than a
laboured address. "Simplicity is always impressive. They were four
words which God caused to be written on the wall amid Belshazzar's
impious revelry; *Mene, mene, tekel, upharsin.* We all remember the
touching history of Jesus the son of Anan, an unlettered rustic, who,
'four years before the war, when Jerusalem was in complete peace and
affluence,' burst in on the people at the feast of tabernacles with one
oft-repeated cry, 'A voice from the East, a voice from the West,
a voice from the four winds, a voice on Jerusalem and the temple, a
voice on the bridegrooms and the brides, a voice on the whole people;'
how he went about through all the lanes of the city, repeating, day and
night, this one cry; and when scourged until his bones were laid bare,
echoed every lash with 'Woe, woe, to Jerusalem,' and continued as his
daily dirge and his one response to daily good or ill-treatment, 'Woe,
woe, to Jerusalem.' The magistrates and even the cold Josephus
thought that there was something in it above nature." (Pusey.)

5—10.　*The happy Result of Jonah's Preaching.*

So the people of Nineveh believed God, and pro- 5
claimed a fast, and put on sackcloth, from the greatest
of them even to the least of them. For word came unto 6

5—10.　THE HAPPY RESULT OF JONAH'S PREACHING.

5. *believed God*] Or, **believed in God.** Three things their faith
certainly embraced. They believed in the God of the Hebrews, as
the true God. They believed in His power to execute the threat which
He had held out. They believed in His mercy and willingness to
forgive the penitent. And this was marvellous faith in heathen, con-
trasting favourably with that of the chosen people. "So great faith"
had not been found, "no not in Israel." What they knew of the
Hebrews and their God (for doubtless they recognised in Jonah a *Jewish*
prophet) may have contributed to the result. That they knew also the
miraculous history of Jonah's mission to them, and so were the better
prepared to credit him, appears to be plainly taught us by our Lord.
It is difficult to understand how Jonah should have been "a sign unto
the Ninevites," corresponding in any way to the sign, which by His
resurrection the "Son of man" was to "the men of that generation,"
(Luke xi. 30 with Matthew xii. 38—41,) unless they were aware that
he had passed, as it were, through death to life again, on his way to
preach to them. How that information reached them we have no
means of judging certainly. Of course it may have come to them
from the lips of Jonah himself, though we have seen reason (see note
on *v.* 4) to regard that as improbable. Alford speaks of "his preaching
after his resurrection to the Ninevites, announcing (for that would necessarily be involved in that preaching) the wonderful judgment of God in
bringing him there, and thus making his own deliverance, that he might
preach to them, *a sign* to that people."

6. *For word came unto*] Rather, **And the tidings reached,** R.V.
The introduction of the word "for" for "and" in A.V. is of the nature of
a gloss. Our translators appear to have taken the view that *v.* 5
states *generally* the effect of Jonah's preaching upon the Ninevites,
and that *vv.* 6—9 relate more particularly how the fast mentioned
in *v.* 5 was brought about. "They proclaimed a fast," I said, "and
it was by a royal edict that they did so, *for* the report of what was
going on was brought to the king, and he too was moved like his
people, and both inaugurated in his own person and instituted by his
authority a national fast." The statement in *v.* 5, however, is not necessarily proleptical. It may be intended by the writer to describe the
effect produced in each district of the city as Jonah reached it, *before* the
Court had any knowledge of what was going on. The people were
first impressed, and then their rulers. The tide of penitence and humiliation rose higher and higher, till it reached and included the king
and his nobles, and what had been done by spontaneous action, or local
authority, received the final sanction and imprimatur of the central

the king of Nineveh, and he arose from his throne, and
he laid his robe from him, and covered *him* with sack-
7 cloth, and sat in ashes. And he caused *it* to be pro-

government. Whichever view be adopted, the literal translation should
be retained.

he arose from his throne, &c.] It is in favour of the view that the
people did not wait for the royal edict to commence their fast, that the
king himself seems to have been the subject of immediate and strong
emotion, as soon as the tidings reached him. He first, as by a resistless
impulse, humbled himself to the dust, and then took measures, out of
the depth of his humiliation, that his subjects should be humbled with
him.

The outward form which the humiliation both of king and people
took was that common in the East (comp. Ezek. xxvi. 16; and see
Dictionary of the Bible, Article *Mourning*), as we know both from sacred
and secular writings. In the case of the king of Assyria it is the
more remarkable both because of his characteristic pride as "the great
king" (2 Kings xviii. 19, 28), and because of the pomp and luxury with
which he was ordinarily surrounded. No greater contrast could well
be conceived than between the royal "robe" and "sackcloth," or between the heap of "ashes" and the king's "throne." "In the bas-
relief I am describing," writes Layard, "the dress of a king consisted
of a long flowing garment, edged with fringes and tassels, descending to
his ankles, and confined at the waist by a girdle. Over this robe a
second, similarly ornamented and open in front, appears to have been
thrown. From his shoulders fell a cape or hood, also adorned with
tassels, and to it were attached two long ribbons or lappets. He wore
the conical mitre, or tiara, which distinguishes the monarch in Assyrian
bas-reliefs, and appears to have been reserved for him alone.......Around
the neck of the king was a necklace. He wore ear-rings, and his arms,
which were bare from a little above the elbow, were encircled by armlets
and bracelets remarkable for the beauty of their forms. The clasps
were formed by the heads of animals, and the centre by stars and
rosettes, probably inlaid with precious stones." (*Nineveh*, abridged
edition, 1851, p. 97.)

Of the throne the same writer says, "The thrones or arm-chairs, supported by animals and human figures, resemble those of the ancient
Egyptians, and of the monuments of Kouyunjik, Khorsabad and Per-
sepolis. They also remind us of the throne of Solomon, which had
'stays (or arms) on either side on the place of the seat, *and two lions
stood by the stays*. And twelve lions stood there, on the one side and on
the other, upon the six steps.'" 1 Kings x. 19, 20. (*Ib.* p. 164.)

his robe] The same word is used of Achan's "goodly Babylonish
garment," Josh. vii. 21, which this may have resembled. But it is also
used of a garment of rough hair-cloth, Gen. xxv. 25; Zech. xiii. 4, and
of Elijah's hairy "mantle," or cloak, 1 Kings xix. 13, 19. The root-
meaning of the word is size, amplitude.

claimed and published through Nineveh by the decree of
the king and his nobles, saying, Let neither man nor beast,
herd nor flock, taste any thing: let them not feed, nor drink

7. *and published*] This word is not a participle, though likely to
be taken for one in the A. V. It is literally, "**And he caused a proclamation to be made, and said,** &c.

the decree] The word here used is not properly a Hebrew word. It
occurs frequently in the Chaldee of Daniel and Ezra to denote a
mandate or decree of the Babylonish and Persian monarchs. Dr
Pusey rightly sees in the employment of it here a proof of the
"accuracy" of Jonah as a writer. He observes, "This is a Syriac
word; and accordingly, since it has now been ascertained beyond all question that the language of Nineveh was a dialect of Syriac, it was, with
a Hebrew pronunciation (the vowel points are different here from
those in Daniel and Ezra), the very word used of this decree at
Nineveh."

and his nobles] Lit., **his great men**, or grandees, Prov. xviii. 16.
We have a similar association of his nobles with himself by Darius the
Mede, when he caused the stone which was laid upon the mouth of the
den, into which Daniel had been cast, to be sealed "with his own signet
and with the signet of his lords, that the purpose might not be changed
concerning Daniel" (Dan. vi. 17). In the present case, however, it
would seem that it was not in the exercise of a constitutional right, but
by a voluntary act on the part of the king, that the nobles were
associated with him in the edict which he issued. Kalisch observes,
" It would be unsafe to infer from this passage that the nobles were in
some manner constitutionally connected with the government of the
kingdom, and thus tempered its arbitrariness, as we know now from
the monuments, no less than from the records of history, that 'the
Assyrian monarch was a thorough Eastern despot, unchecked by
popular opinion, and having complete power over the lives and property of his subjects, rather adored as a god than feared as a man.'"
(Layard, *Nin. and Babyl.* p. 632). May not this association of his
nobles with himself have been "fruit meet for repentance," an abdica-
tion, in some sort, of the haughty arbitrariness of his power, an humbling
of himself "under the mighty hand of God"?

saying] The decree, thus introduced, extends to the end of *v.* 9.

man nor beast, herd nor flock] The Hebrew word for " beast " here
means tame or domestic animals, and probably refers only to "beasts of
burden," horses, mules, and the like. So Ahab says to Obadiah
when the famine was in Samaria, "peradventure we may find grass to
save the horses and mules alive, that we be not deprived of beasts"
(1 Kings xviii. 5). "Herd and flock" will then be an additional clause,
not amplifying, but distinct from " beast," and the covering with
sackcloth, in *v.* 8, will thus be confined to those animals which were in
man's more immediate use, and many of which, with their gay and costly
trappings and harness, had been the ministers of his pomp and pride,
or, as employed in war, had been the instruments of his "violence."

8 water: but let man and beast be covered with sackcloth, and
cry mightily unto God: yea, let them turn every one from his

The extension of the fast to all, and of the sackcloth to some at least, of
the animals in Nineveh, is probably without exact parallel in extant history.
The *Speaker's Commentary* rightly points out that "the *voluntary* fasting of animals, wild as well as tame, at the death of Daphnis, described
by Virgil, *Eclog.* v. 24—28, which has often been referred to, is plainly
a mere poetic fancy." But the description in the text is quite in keeping
with the common instinct and practice of mankind. Men have always
been wont to extend the outward signs of their joy or sorrow to everything under their control. Our dress, our food, our houses, our equipage,
our horses, our servants, all wear the hue of the occasion for which
they are employed. "Man, in his luxury and pride, would have
everything reflect his glory and minister to pomp. Self-humiliation
would have everything reflect its lowliness. Sorrow would have everything answer to its sorrow. Men think it strange that the horses at
Nineveh were covered with sackcloth, and forget how, at the funerals
of the rich, black horses are chosen, and are clothed with black velvet"
(Pusey). In the extreme case of Nineveh, the instinct may well have
been indulged to an extreme. Like all other common instincts of our
nature, it had a true origin, for the destiny of man and of the lower
creation is inseparably connected (Gen. i. 26, 28; Rom. viii. 19—23).
The effect upon the Ninevites of seeing "their deserts set before them
as in a mirror or a picture" (Calvin), all that belonged to them involved
with them, through their guilt, in a common danger with themselves—
all creation, as it were, threatened and humbled for the sin of its
lord—may well have been to incite them powerfully to repentance.
The appeal to the compassion of Almighty God, who "preserveth man
and beast" (Ps. xxxvi. 6; comp. ch. iv. 11), may well have been
strengthened by the mute misery of the innocent beasts (Joel i. 20)
But, apart from these considerations, the requirements of the history are
fully satisfied by regarding the act of the king of Nineveh as instinctive,
called for by the urgent circumstances of the case, and coloured by the
demonstrativeness of oriental character.

8. *and cry mightily*] These words are to be restricted to "man."
They do not include, as some have thought (comparing Joel i. 18, 20),
"beast" as well. The addition "mightily" favours the restriction, and
so also does the exact order of the Hebrew: "Let them be clothed
with sackcloth, man and beast (the parenthesis is inserted here as
qualifying what precedes only), and let them cry......and let them
turn," &c.

let them turn] The prominence of the moral element in the repentance of heathen Nineveh is very striking. Complete as was the outward act of humiliation, the king's decree implies that it would be
worthless without a corresponding moral reformation. The tenth verse
tells us that it was to this that God had respect, "He saw their works,
that they turned from their evil way," and the heathen king seems
clearly to have understood that it would be so. Here again, the favour-

evil way, and from the violence that *is* in their hands. Who 9
can tell *if* God will turn and repent, and turn away from his

able light in which these heathen show, in comparison with the chosen
people, is most marked. Frequent and indignant is the remonstrance
of the Hebrew prophets against the attempt of their countrymen to
gain the favour or avert the displeasure of Almighty God by fasting
and sackcloth, while the heart remained unchanged and the life un-
renewed. "Is it such a fast that I have chosen?" is God's own
indignant question to His people by the prophet Isaiah (ch. lviii.).

the violence that is in their hands] "Violence" was their chief sin,
as all we learn of the Assyrians, both from sacred and secular history,
shows. Comp. Nahum ii. 11, 12, iii. 1, and Isaiah x. 13, 14. The form
of expression, *in their hands*, the hand being the instrument of violence,
is the same as in Ps. vii. 3 (Heb. 4), and elsewhere.

9. *Who can tell*] Comp. Joel ii. 14, where the Hebrew is the
same. Calvin well explains the doubtful form assumed by the king's
decree. "How can it be," he asks, "that the king of Nineveh repented earnestly and unfeignedly, and yet spoke doubtfully of the
grace of God?" I answer, that there is a kind of doubt which may be
associated with faith; that, namely, which does not directly reject the
promise of God, but which has other things as well in view....... No
doubt the king of Nineveh conceived the hope of deliverance, but in
the mean time he was still perplexed in mind, both on account of
the preaching of Jonah, and on account of his consciousness of his own
sins...... The first obstacle (to his immediate certainty of forgiveness) was
that dreadful preaching, Nineveh after forty days shall perish....... Then
again, the king, no doubt when he pondered his sins might well waver
a little."

God will turn] Lit., **the God**, i. e. the One supreme God. See note
on i. 6, and comp. 1 Kings xviii. 39. This acknowledgment by the
Assyrians of Jehovah, the God of the Jews, as "the God" is all the
more remarkable, because, as Kalisch points out (though he unhappily
sees in the description of this chapter, not an historical fact, magnifying
the grace of God and the efficacy of true repentance, but the "aspiration"
of a later writer for "that time when 'the Lord shall be One and His
name One'"), it is contrary to all else we know of them. "The prophet
Nahum declares distinctly, among other menaces pronounced against
Nineveh, 'Out of the house of thy gods will I cut off the graven image
and the molten image' (i. 14; comp. iii. 4); the Books of Kings state
by name the Eastern idols Nibhaz and Tartak, Nergal and Ashima,
Adrammelech and Anammelech (2 Kings xvii. 30, 31); in the remarkable account of Sennacherib's war against Hezekiah, the former,
through the mouth of one of his chief officers, bitterly taunts the Hebrew
king with his futile reliance on his national god, whose nature the
Assyrian understands so little that, in his opinion, Hezekiah must have
incurred Jahveh's wrath, for having deprived him of all the heights and
of all the altars except that solitary one in Jerusalem; and he places, in
fact, Jahveh on the same level of power with the gods of Hamath and

10 fierce anger, that we perish not?   And God saw their works,
that they turned from their evil way; and God repented of

Arpad, or any Syrian idol (2 Kings xviii. 22, 30, 33, 34). And, on the
other hand, all Assyrian monuments and records, whether of a date
earlier or later than Jeroboam II., disclose the same vast pantheon
which was the boast of king and people alike—Asshur, 'the great lord
ruling supreme over all the gods,' with his twelve greater and four
thousand inferior deities presiding over all manifestations of nature and
all complications of human life ; for the Assyrians at all times saw their
strength and their bulwark in the *multitude* of their gods, and considered
that nation feeble and defenceless indeed, which enjoyed only the pro-
tection of a single divinity."

10. *that they turned from their evil way*]   "See what removed that
inevitable wrath. Did fasting and sackcloth alone? No, but the
change of the whole life. How does this appear? From the prophet's
word itself. For he who spake of the wrath of God and of their fast,
himself mentions the reconciliation and its cause. *And God saw their
works.* What works? that they fasted? that they put on sackcloth?
He passes by these and says, *that everyone turned from his evil ways ;
and God repented of the evil which He had said that He would do
unto them.*   Seest thou that not the fast plucked them from the peril,
but the change of life made God propitious to these heathen? I say
this, not that we should dishonour, but that we may honour fasting.
For the honour of a fast is not in abstinence from food, but in avoid-
ance of sin. So that he who limiteth fasting to the abstinence from
food only, he it is who above all dishonoureth it. Fastest thou? Show
it me by thy works." St Chrysostom, *On the Statues*, Hom. iii. 4,
quoted by Pusey.

God repented] When we regard the relations of Almighty God to
men and His dealings with them *from the divine side*, so far as it
is revealed to us and we are able to comprehend it, then they are all
foreseen and planned and executed in accordance with His perfect fore-
knowledge.   Then there is no place for repentance, no room for
change. "Known unto God are all His works from the beginning of
the world." But when we alter our stand-point, and regard them *from
the human side*, when from the pure heights of contemplation we come
down to the busy field of action, free scope is given in the aspect
in which God then presents Himself to us for human effort and prayer
and feeling, then His purpose waits upon our will. Both of these
sides are freely and fearlessly set forth in Holy Scripture. On the one
side, "God is not a man that He should lie, neither the son of man
that He should repent" (Num. xxiii. 19). With Him "is no variable-
ness, neither shadow of turning " (James i. 17). On the other side we
read, "It repented the Lord that He had made man on the earth, and
it grieved Him at His heart" (Gen. vi. 6); "God repented of the evil
that He had said that He would do unto them, and He did it not."
Both views are equally true, and they are in perfect harmony with each
other, but Holy Scripture never attempts to harmonise them, nor is it

the evil, that he had said that he would do unto them; and
he did *it* not.

1—11. *Jonah's Displeasure, and its Rebuke.*

Dut it displeased Jonah exceedingly, and he was very 4

wise for us to attempt to do so; we cannot look upon both sides of the
shield at once.

he did it not] It is obvious that this statement, and indeed the whole
account of the repentance of the Ninevites, is to be taken within the
limits which the history itself prescribes. There is nothing here to
contradict the subsequent relapse of the Ninevites into sin, their filling
up the measures of their iniquities, and the consequent overthrow of
their city and extinction of their national life. But none of these
things are here in view, the present fills the whole picture, and fills it
grandly. They are sinners. They are threatened. They repent. They
are saved.

The fact that no reference has been discovered amongst extant
Assyrian monuments to the mission of Jonah and its results may be
reasonably accounted for. The Assyrian records of this particular
period are singularly meagre in comparison of those of the immediately
preceding and succeeding reigns. The subject-matter of this event in
the national history is not such as the monuments are wont to record.
Wars and victories and material works chiefly occupy them. Moral
reformation is foreign to their theme. The marvellous manner in which
recent discoveries have come in confirmation of the statements of Holy
Scripture leave it open to us, however, to believe that some such
confirmation of the history of Jonah may yet reach us from secular
sources.

CH. IV. 1—11. JONAH'S DISPLEASURE, AND ITS REBUKE.

Greatly displeased at the clemency of God towards Nineveh, Jonah
confesses that it was the expectation that that clemency would be exercised, which rendered him unwilling to undertake the divine mission at
the first, and in his annoyance and chagrin requests that he may die,
1—3. Met by the calm appeal to reason, which however he is in no
mood to entertain, *Doest thou well to be angry?* Jonah goes out of the
city, and constructs in the immediate vicinity a booth or hut, under
the shelter of which he may dwell and watch, till the forty days are
expired, what the fate of Nineveh will be, 4, 5. Intending to correct
and instruct him by an acted parable, in which he himself should bear
the chief part, God causes a wide-spreading plant to spring up and
cover his booth with its refreshing shade. But scarcely has Jonah
begun to enjoy the welcome shelter from the burning rays of the sun
thus afforded him, when God, in pursuit of His lesson, causes the plant

2 angry. And he prayed unto the LORD, and said, I pray

to be attacked by insects, which rapidly strip it of its protecting leaves
and cause it to wither away, 6, 7.   Once again, the hand that governs
all things sets in motion, like the blast of a furnace, the burning wind
of the desert, and the sun's unbroken rays pour down on the now defenceless head of Jonah, so that faint and weary, beneath the weight of
bodily distress and mental disappointment, he urges anew his pas-
sionate complaint, *Better for me to die than to live!* 7, 8.   And now
the parable is complete, and only needs to be applied and interpreted.
Thou couldst have pity upon a short-lived plant, which cost thee and
which owed thee nothing ; thou art angry and justifiest thine anger,
even unto death, for its loss ; and shall not I, the Maker and the Lord
of all, have pity upon a great city, which, apart from its adult population who might seem to have deserved their doom, numbers its sixscore thousand innocent children, and "very much cattle"—they too
"much better than" a plant? 9—11.
    1. *it displeased Jonah, &c.*] Lit. **It was evil to Jonah, a great
evil, and it** (viz. anger) **kindled to him.** Comp. Nehem. ii. 10.   It
is clear that the immediate cause of Jonah's anger and vexation was the
preservation of Nineveh and the non-fulfilment of the threat which he
had been sent to pronounce.   It was the anticipation of this result,
founded on the revealed character of God, that made him decline the
errand at first (*v.* 2).   It was the realisation of it that so greatly troubled
him now.   But why this result of his mission should have thus affected
him it has not been found so easy to decide.   Some have thought—but
the view has nothing to commend it—that his annoyance was purely
personal and selfish, and that he was stung by the disgrace of appearing
as a false prophet in the sight of the heathen because his predictions
had not been verified.   Others with better show of reason have assigned
to his displeasure the more worthy motive of jealousy for the honour
of God, in whose name and with whose message he had come to
Nineveh, and on whom he thought the reproach of fickleness and in-
constancy would fall.   "He connected," writes Calvin, "his own
ministry with the glory of God, and rightly, because it depended on His
authority.   Jonah, when he entered Nineveh, did not utter his cry as a
private individual, but professed himself to be sent by God.   Now, if the
proclamation of Jonah is found to be false, the disgrace will fall upon
the author of the call himself, namely on God.   There is no doubt,
therefore, that Jonah took it ill that the name of God was exposed to
the revilings of the heathen, as though He terrified without cause."
It is far more satisfactory, however, to suppose that Jonah was displeased that the mercy of God should be extended to heathen, and
especially to heathen who were the enemies and future oppressors of his
own people, and that he himself should be the messenger of that
mercy.   This view falls in entirely with the exclusive spirit which marks
the Old Testament dispensation, while it brings out into bold relief the
liberal and Catholic spirit of the New Testament, which it is the object
of this book to inculcate.

thee, O LORD, *was* not this my saying, when I was yet in my country? Therefore I fled before unto Tarshish : for I knew that thou *art* a gracious God, and merciful, slow to anger, and of great kindness, and repentest thee of the evil. Therefore 3 now, O LORD, take, I beseech thee, my life from me; for *it is* better for me to die than to live. Then said the LORD, ↓

2. *he prayed*] His better mind had not altogether forsaken him. He did not as before flee from the presence of the Lord, but betook himself to Him, even in his irritation and discontent.

I pray thee] A particle of entreaty. In I. 14 it is translated "we beseech thee."

I fled before] Lit. **I prevented or anticipated to flee.** That is, *I fled before something could happen.* LXX. προέφθασα τοῦ φυγεῖν. The ellipsis has been variously supplied. "'I anticipated or prevented (another charge) by escaping'; that is 'I fled before' another charge could reach me."—Kalisch. "I anticipated (the danger which threatens me) by fleeing to Tarshish."—Gesenius. "I hastened my flight."—Rosenmüller; or, "hasted to flee," R.V.

for I knew, &c.] In common with all Israelites Jonah knew the character of God to be what he here describes it, from His ancient revelation to Moses (Exodus xxxiv. 6), repeated frequently by prophets and psalmists (Numbers xiv. 18; Psalm ciii. 8, cxlv. 8), and renewed in exactly the same terms as here by the prophet Joel (ii. 13). Knowing that God threatens that He may spare, and warns that He may save, Jonah rightly understood from the first that his mission to Nineveh was a mission of mercy, and therefore he was unwilling to undertake it.

3. *take...my life from me*] So had Moses prayed (Numbers xi. 15) and Elijah (1 Kings xix. 4), both with better cause, and in nobler spirit, but both in the same utter weariness of life as Jonah. No one of them, however, attempts to take his own life. They all regard it as a sacred deposit, entrusted to them by God and only to be relinquished at His bidding, or in accordance with His will. Comp. *v.* 8 below.

4. *Doest thou well to be angry?*] Two other translations of these words have been suggested. One, which though perhaps possible is far-fetched and highly improbable, is, "Does (my) doing good (that is, to Nineveh in sparing it) make thee angry?" the reproof then being similar to that in Matthew xx. 15, "Is thine eye evil because I am good?" The other, which is given in the margin both of A.V. and R.V., "Art thou greatly angry?" is fully borne out by the Hebrew, but, as has been truly said, it "is in this context almost pointless." But the rendering of the text is in accordance with Hebrew usage (comp. "They have well said all that they have spoken," Deut. v. 28 [Heb. 25]; "Thou hast well seen," Jer. i. 12) and gives a much more forcible sense. It is the gentle question of suggested reproof, designed to still the tumult of passion and lead to consideration and reflection. God does not as a judge condemn Jonah's unreasonable anger, but invites him to judge and condemn himself.

5 Doest thou well to be angry? So Jonah went out of the
city, and sat on the east side of the city, and there made him
a booth, and sat under it in the shadow, till he might see
6 what would become of the city. And the LORD God pre-

5. *So Jonah went out of the city*] It has been proposed to take the
verbs in this verse as pluperfects: "Now Jonah had gone out of the
city, and abode on the east side of the city, &c." The verse will then
be a parenthesis introduced to relate what had really taken place before
Jonah's anger and complaint. In point of time it will precede the first
verse of the chapter. It is doubtful, however, whether such a rendering is grammatically allowable; nor is there any reason for adopting
it. The course of the narrative flows regularly on throughout the chapter. Jonah while still in the city comes to know that Nineveh will be
spared. In bitter displeasure he complains to God, and is rebuked
(*vv.* 1—4). Still cherishing the hope of vengeance, fostered possibly
by the question in *v.* 4, which his distempered mind might interpret
to mean, "Do not judge too hastily what My purposes may be," he
will not abandon the city altogether. He will linger yet awhile in its
precincts, and watch what its fate shall be.

on the east side of the city] where it was skirted by hills. Probably
he chose some eminence from which he could command a view of the
city.

a booth] of twigs and branches, such as the Israelites were directed to
dwell in for seven days at the feast of tabernacles (Lev. xxiii. 42; Neh.
viii. 14—16). Such were the "tabernacles" which St Peter proposed
to make on the Mount of Transfiguration.

till he might see what would become of the city] We are not told whether this was before or after the forty days had expired. If it was
before, then we must suppose that Jonah, and possibly the Ninevites
also, had some direct intimation that God would spare the city, and
that Jonah in his reluctance to accept the result still tarried in the
neighbourhood, in the hope that on the appointed day the blow would
fall. If however we suppose that the forty days had elapsed without
the threatened judgment being executed, and that it was by this that
Jonah and the Ninevites knew that God had repented Him of the evil,
we can only conclude that Jonah hoped for some later punishment upon
the people of Nineveh, provoked it might be by their speedy relapse
into sin. "The days being now past, after which it was time that
the things foretold should be accomplished, and His anger as yet taking
no effect, Jonah understood that a respite of the evil has been granted
them, on their willingness to repent, but thinks that some effect of His
displeasure would come, since the pains of their repentance had not
equalled their offences. So thinking in himself apparently, he departs
from the city, and waits to see what will become of them."—St Cyr.
quoted by Pusey.

6. *prepared*] Rather, **appointed.** And so in *vv.* 7, 8. See i.
17, note.

pared a gourd, and made *it* to come up over Jonah, that *it*

a gourd] This is the only place in the Old Testament in which the
Hebrew word here translated *gourd* occurs. It is quite a different word
which is rendered *gourd* in 2 Kings iv. 39, and (of architectural orna-
ments) in 1 Kings vi. 18 (margin), vii. 24. It is an old controversy,
dating back as far as the times of Jerome and Augustine, whether
Jonah's plant was a gourd or not. It is now generally admitted that it
was not, but that the plant intended is the *ricinus communis* or castor-
oil plant. This plant satisfies all the requirements of the history. The
name *kikayon* here used in the Hebrew is akin to the word *kikeia*
or *kiki* (Herodot. II. 94), which ancient authors tell us was used by the
Egyptians and others for the castor-oil plant. That plant is a native
of North Africa, Arabia, Syria and Palestine, and is said by travellers
to grow abundantly and to a great size in the neighbourhood of the
Tigris. It is succulent, with a hollow stem, and has broad vine-like
leaves (much larger, however, than those of the vine), which from their
supposed resemblance to the extended palm of the hand have gained
for the plant the name of *Palma Christi*, or palmchrist. It grows with
such extraordinary rapidity that under favourable conditions it rises to
about eight feet within five or six months, while in America it has been
known to reach the height of thirteen feet in less than three months.
Jerome also bears testimony to the rapidity of its growth. It is, he
says, "a shrub with broad leaves like vine-leaves. It gives a very
dense shade, and supports itself on its own stem. It grows most abundantly in Palestine, especially in sandy spots. If you cast the seed into
the ground, it is soon quickened, rises marvellously into a tree, and in
a few days what you had beheld a herb you look up to a shrub."—
Pusey.

made it to come up] Or, **it came up.** The naturally rapid growth of
the plant was miraculously accelerated. As in other miracles of Holy
Scripture Almighty God at once resembled nature and exceeded nature. "We know that God, when He does anything beyond the course
of nature, does nevertheless come near to nature in His working.
This is not indeed always the case; but we shall find for the
most part that God has so worked as to outdo the course of
nature, and yet not to desert nature altogether.... So too in this place,
I do not doubt that God chose a plant, which would quickly grow up
even to such a height as this, and yet that He surpassed the wonted
course of nature." (Calvin.) In like manner, our Lord, when at the
marriage-feast in Cana He turned the water into wine, "was working
in the line of (above, indeed, but not across or counter to) His more
ordinary workings, which we see daily around us, the unnoticed
miracles of every-day nature." "He made wine that day at the mar-
riage in those six water-pots which He had commanded to be filled with
water, Who every year makes it in the vines. For as what the servants
had put into the water-pots was turned into wine by the working of the
Lord, so too what the clouds pour forth is turned into wine by the working of the same Lord. This however, we do not wonder at, because it

might be a shadow over his head, to deliver him from his
7 grief. So Jonah was exceeding glad of the gourd. But God
prepared a worm when the morning rose the next day, and
8 it smote the gourd, that it withered. And it came to pass,
when the sun did arise, that God prepared a vehement east

happens every year: its frequency has made it cease to be a marvel."
St Augustine, quoted by Trench *On the Miracles.*

a shadow over his head] His booth or hut, made as we have seen of
twigs and branches, the leaves of which would naturally soon wither,
was far from being impervious to the rays of the sun. The living plant
rising above the booth and covering it with its broad shadow would
prove a most welcome addition.

from his grief] Lit. **his evil**, the same word as in *v.* 1. The gloomy
and dissatisfied condition of his mind had been aggravated by physical
causes. The heat and closeness of his booth had added to the weariness
and oppression of his spirit. The palmchrist with its refreshing shade
by ministering to his bodily comfort had tended also to calm and soothe
the agitation of his mind. We need not look for any deeper meaning
in the words. It is surely a mistake to say that Jonah "must have
looked upon its sudden growth as a fruit of God's goodness towards
him (as it was) and then perhaps went on to think (as people do) that
this favour of God showed that He meant in the end to grant him
what his heart was set upon." (Pusey.) The object of the writer is
not to tell us what inferences Jonah drew from the sudden growth of the
plant, but what was the object and intention of Almighty God in
causing it to grow up over him. He sent it to refresh him as a step in
His lesson of correction and amendment; He did not send it to mislead
him. The force of the rebuke in verses 10, 11, in which the chapter
culminates and which turns entirely upon Jonah's joy and grief for the
plant, is greatly weakened if we import into that joy and grief such
moral elements.

7. *a worm*] This of course may mean a single worm which either
by attacking the root or gnawing the stem, still young and tender and
not yet hardened by maturity, suddenly destroyed the palmchrist. It
is better, however, to take the word in its collective sense, *worms*, as in
Deut. xxviii. 39; Isaiah xiv. 11, and other passages. Thus the special
intervention of Almighty God again accommodates itself to nature.
"The destruction may have been altogether in the way of nature,
except that it happened at that precise moment, when it was to be
a lesson to Jonah. 'On warm days, when a small rain falls, black
caterpillars are generated in great numbers on this plant, which, in one
night, so often and so suddenly cut off its leaves, that only their bare
ribs remain, which I have often observed with much wonder, as though
it were a copy of that destruction of old at Nineveh.' "—Pusey.

8. *a vehement east wind*] Margin, *silent.* This, or *sultry*, R.V., is probably the true meaning of the word. "We have two kinds of sirocco,"
writes Dr Thomson, "one accompanied with vehement wind which

wind; and the sun beat upon the head of Jonah, that he
fainted, and wished in himself to die, and said, *It is* better

fills the air with dust and fine sand......The sirocco to-day is of the
quiet kind, and they are often more overpowering than the others.
I encountered one a year ago on my way from Lydd to Jerusalem.
There is no living thing abroad to make a noise. The birds hide in
thickest shades; the fowls pant under the walls with open mouth and
drooping wings; the flocks and herds take shelter in caves and under
great rocks; the labourers retire from the fields, and close the windows
and doors of their houses; and travellers hasten, as I did, to take
shelter in the first cool place they can find. No one has energy enough
to make a noise, and the very air is too weak and languid to stir the
pendent leaves of the tall poplars." *Land and Book*, pp. 536, 537.
The occurrence of this wind at sunrise is referred to as a usual thing
by St James, i. 11, where the same Greek word (καύσων) is used for
"burning heat" as is used by the LXX. here.

fainted] It is the same word as occurs in Genesis xxxviii. 14,
"*covered her with a veil*," veiled herself, the reference being either
to the film that comes over the eyes in fainting and exhaustion, or to
the clouding of the mental powers from the same cause. This word is
used again of fainting from thirst in Amos viii. 13, and a similar word
in the same metaphorical sense in ch. ii. 7 of this book, where see
note.

wished in himself to die] Lit. **asked for his life to die.** Exactly the
same expression occurs with reference to Elijah when he was fleeing from
the wrath of Jezebel, 1 Kings xix. 4. The meaning of the phrase
seems to be that the prophet, both in the one case and in the other,
recognizing that his life was not his own, but God's, asked for it of
Him as a gift or boon, that he might do with it what he pleased.
Then the object with which he asked for it, the way in which he would
have it disposed of, is expressed by the word "to die," or "for death."
Hezekiah might have asked for his life, as indeed he did, in his grievous
sickness, but it was not "to die," but "to live." The example of
Elijah may perhaps have been in Jonah's mind when he penned these
words, or even when he gave vent to his impatient desire to die. If
the Jewish tradition that Jonah was the son of the widow of Zarephath
and the "servant" whom he left at Beersheba, 1 Kings xix. 3, could be
accepted, this would be the more probable. The cases of the two
prophets were however in reality very different. Both were weary of
life. Both desired to die. Both gave expression to their desire in the
same words. But here the resemblance ends. Elijah's was a noble
disappointment. "On Carmel the great object for which Elijah had
lived seemed on the point of being realised. Baal's prophets were
slain, Jehovah acknowledged with one voice : false worship put down.
Elijah's life aim—the transformation of Israel into a kingdom of
God—was all but accomplished. In a single day all this bright picture
was annihilated." (Robertson.) But Jonah's was a far less worthy grief.

₉ for me to die than to live.   And God said to Jonah, Doest
thou well to be angry for the gourd?   And he said, I do well
₁₀ to be angry, *even* unto death.   Then said the LORD, Thou hast

It was not that God's kingdom was overthrown in Israel, but that it
was extended to the heathen world, that made him weary of his life.
Elijah grieved because he had failed in his efforts to convert and save
Israel; Jonah because he had succeeded in converting and saving
Nineveh.

It is better &c.]   The words " *It is* " which, as the italics in A. V.
show, are not in the original, are better omitted : " *And said, Better
for me to die than to live.*"

The excess of Jonah's joy and grief over the bestowal and loss of
the gourd was partly due to his sanguine and impulsive character.
But the influence here ascribed to physical circumstances over the mind,
especially when it is burdened with a great grief, is very true to nature.
" We would fain believe that the mind has power over the body, but
it is just as true that the body rules the mind.   Causes apparently
the most trivial : a heated room—want of exercise—a sunless day—
a northern aspect—will make all the difference between happiness and
unhappiness, between faith and doubt, between courage and indecision."
(Robertson.)

9.   *even unto death*]   " *Art thou rightly angry for the palmchrist?
I am rightly angry, (and that) unto death:*" i. e. " my anger is so great
that it well-nigh kills me, and even in that excess it is justified by the
circumstances."   In like manner it is said of Samson that " his soul was
vexed unto death " by the urgency of Delilah (Judges xvi. 16), and
our Lord exclaims in the garden, " My soul is exceeding sorrowful,
even unto death " (Matt. xxvi. 38), where Alford observes, " Our
Lord's soul was crushed down even to death by the weight of that
anguish which lay upon Him—and that *literally*—so that He (as regards
His humanity) *would have died*, had not strength (*bodily* strength up-
holding His human frame) been ministered from on high by an angel,
Luke xxii. 43."   The question in its more general form, " Doest thou
well to be angry?" (*v.* 4) is here narrowed to a single issue, " Doest
thou well to be angry *for the palmchrist?*"   And Jonah, in his un-
reasoning irritation, accepts and answers it on that single issue, and
thus unwittingly prepares the way for the unanswerable argument
which follows.

10, 11.]   The final appeal is forcible and conclusive, a grand and
worthy climax to this remarkable book.   The contrasts are striking and
designed : **Thou** and **I** (the pronouns are emphatic, and each of them
introduces a member of the comparison), man and God ; the short-lived
palmchrist and Nineveh that great city ; the plant that cost thee nothing,
the vast population, the sixscore thousand children, the very much cattle,
which I made and uphold continually.   Jonah is met upon his own
ground, the merely human sentiment of compassion, regard for what
is useful and good after its kind, sorrow for its loss, unwillingness to
see it perish.   The higher moral ground is for the time abandoned.

had pity on the gourd, for the which thou hast not laboured,
neither madest it grow; which came up in a night, and
perished in a night: and should not I spare Nineveh, *that* 11
great city, wherein are more than sixscore thousand persons
that cannot discern between their right hand and their left
hand; and *also* much cattle?

The repentance of the Ninevites is not brought into consideration.
But the lower ground is a step to the higher. "The natural God-
implanted feeling is the germ of the spiritual."

10. *for the which thou hast not laboured, neither madest it grow*]
The principle on which the contrast implied by these words rests
is that the effort which we have bestowed upon any object, the degree
in which our powers of mind or heart or body have been expended
upon it, in a word what it has cost us, is a measure of our regard for it.
No claim of this kind had the plant on Jonah. No single effort had
he made for it. He had not planted, or trained, or watered it, yet
he pitied it, and mourned for its decay with a yearning tenderness.
But on Almighty God, though the contrast is rather implied than
expressed, all creation has such a claim in fullest measure. He
"labours" not indeed ; He speaks, and it is done; He wills, and it is
accomplished. Yet in all things that exist He has the deepest interest.
He planned them, He made them, He sustains them, He rules them,
He cares for them. His tender mercies are over all His works. "This
entire train of thought," as Kalisch well remarks, "is implied in the
following fine lines of the Wisdom of Solomon : 'The whole world is
before Thee as a drop of the morning dew ; but Thou hast mercy upon
all......and overlookest the sins of men, in order that they may amend ;
for Thou lovest all the things that are, and disdainest nothing that
Thou hast made. ...Indeed Thou sparest all, for they are Thine, O
Lord, Thou lover of souls.' Wisd. xi. 22—26."

came up in a night &c.] lit. **was the son of a night, and perished
the son of a night,** i.e. it came into existence and reached maturity
(comp. for this sense of *was*, And God said Let light be, and light was,
Gen. i. 3) in a single night, and no less rapidly (not literally in a
single night, for it was when the morning arose) withered away.

11. *that cannot discern &c.*] The idea that the whole population
of Nineveh is thus described, the reference being to their moral condition of heathen ignorance and darkness, has nothing to recommend it.
On the contrary, the moral susceptibility of the Ninevites, although they
are heathen, is, as we have seen, a prominent feature in the history.
The reference is no doubt to the children of tender age who were as
yet incapable of moral discrimination, and could not therefore be
regarded as responsible agents. The same thought is expressed, without a metaphor, by the phrases, "having no knowledge between good
and evil," Deut. i. 39 ; "Knowing to refuse the evil, and choose the
good," Isaiah vii. 15, 16. Between these helpless and innocent children,
together with the great multitude of unoffending animals which the

vast area of Nineveh contained, and the plant over which Jonah mourned, regarded simply as objects of human compassion, all moral considerations apart, the comparison lies.

Any attempt to compute the whole population of Nineveh from the data thus given must necessarily be precarious, from the difficulty of deciding at what age the line is to be drawn. But in any case the total would not be excessive, for the population of so large an area as we have seen that Nineveh enclosed.

NOTE A. THE GREAT FISH.

THERE is no reason to suppose that the fish which swallowed Jonah was not naturally capable of swallowing him whole. The old objection, that it is said to have been a whale, and that the gullet of a whale is not large enough to allow of the passage of a man, rests, as is now generally known, upon a mistake. Jonah's fish is not really said to have been a whale. Even if it were, it might be urged that one kind of whale, " the sperm whale (*Catodon macrocephalus*) has a gullet sufficiently large to admit the body of a man " (Smith's *Bible Dict.*, Art. *Whale*), and that if whales are not now found in the Mediterranean, they may have been "frightened out of it" by the multiplication of ships, and may have been common there in Jonah's time, when "navigation was in its infancy, ships were few and small, and they kept mostly along the shores, leaving the interior undisturbed." (Thomson, *The Land and the Book*, pp. 68, 69.) But in fact the common idea of Jonah being swallowed by a whale has no real warrant in holy Scripture at all. Our Lord, indeed, is made to say in our English Bibles that Jonah was "in the whale's belly" (Matt. xii. 40); but the word ($\kappa\tilde{\eta}\tau\sigma\varsigma$) used by Him to denote Jonah's fish is taken from the Greek translation of the Book of Jonah, with which He and His hearers were familiar, and cannot be restricted to a whale, or to any of the so-called *Cetaceans*. It means "any sea-monster, or huge fish," and is used of a "seal, or sea-calf, and later especially of whales, sharks, and large tunnies." (Liddell and Scott, *Lex.* s. v.). The Bible then does not say that Jonah was swallowed by a whale. The O. T. simply speaks of "a great fish," and the N. T. employs a strictly equivalent term. Here we might be content to leave the question. We are not bound to show what the fish was. It is, however, interesting to enquire whether any particular fish can with probability be fixed upon, and the rather because the choice of an agent ready to hand and naturally fitted for the work accords with that "economy" of the miraculous which is characteristic of holy Scripture. Now it has been satisfactorily proved that the common or white shark (*Carcharias vulgaris*) is found in the Mediterranean, and well-authenticated instances have been given of its having swallowed men and other large animals entire. "A natural historian of repute relates, ' In 1758, in stormy weather, a sailor fell overboard from a frigate in the Mediterranean. A shark was close by, which, as he was swimming and crying for help, took him in his wide throat, so that

he forthwith disappeared. Other sailors had leaped into the sloop, to
help their comrade, while yet swimming; the captain had a gun which
stood on the deck discharged at the fish, which struck it so, that it cast
out the sailor which it had in its throat, who was taken up, alive and
little injured, by the sloop which had now come up. The fish was
harpooned, taken up on the frigate and dried. The captain made a
present of the fish to the sailor who, by God's Providence, had been so
wonderfully preserved. The sailor went round Europe exhibiting it.
He came to Franconia, and it was publicly exhibited here in Erlangen,
as also at Nurnberg and other places. The dried fish was delineated.
It was 20 feet long, and, with expanded fins, nine feet wide, and
weighed 3924 pounds. From all this, it is probable that this was the
fish of Jonah.'" (See Dr Pusey's *Commentary on Jonah*, Introd.,
pp. 257, 258; Smith's *Bible Dict.*, Art. *Whale*, where other instances
are given.) There is another fish, of which the Norwegian name is
Rorqual, i. e. *whale with folds*, which from its peculiar internal con-
struction is thought likely by some commentators to have been the
receptacle of Jonah. "The distinguishing feature of the whole genus
is the possession of 'a number of longitudinal folds, nearly parallel,
which commence under the lower lip, occupying the space between the
two branches of the jaw, pass down the throat, covering the whole
extent of the chest from one fin to the other, and terminate far down
the abdomen;' in the Mediterranean species 'reaching to the vent.'"
It has accordingly been suggested that "it may have been in the folds
of a Rorqual's mouth, which in the case of an individual 75 feet
long (such as was actually stranded at St Cyprien, Eastern Pyrenees,
in 1828) would be a cavity of between 15 and 20 feet in length, that
the prophet was imbedded." (*Speaker's Commentary* in loc., and
Encycl. Brit. quoted there.) It would seem, however, that this Rorqual's throat is not large enough to swallow a man, so that on the
whole it is most likely that Jonah's fish was a shark.

NOTE B. NINEVEH.

It is evidently the design of the writer of this Book to give prominence to the vast size of Nineveh. When he speaks of it, it is with
the constant addition, "*the great city,*" (i. 2; iii. 2; iv. 11), and the
addition is justified by the statements that it was "great to God," that
it was a city "of three days' journey," and that it contained "more than
sixscore thousand persons unable to discern between their right hand
and their left, and also much cattle" (iv. 11). In seeking to verify this
description and to identify, with some reasonable degree of probability,
the Nineveh of Jonah, we have first to determine what is meant by the
expression "a city of three days' journey." It has been held that the
"three days' journey" describes the time that would be occupied in
traversing the city from end to end; along "the 'high street' representing the greatest length or 'the diameter' of the town, which ran
from one principal gate to the opposite extremity." (Kalisch.) But
unless we are prepared to regard the "figures given in the text" as

"the natural hyperboles of a writer who lived long after the virtual destruction of the city, and who, moreover, was anxious to enhance the impressiveness of his story and lesson, by dwelling on the vastness of the population whose fate depended on their moral regeneration" (Ib.), we shall find it difficult to accept the gratuitous assumption that Nineveh is here described as a city "about fifty-five English miles in diameter," with a "high street" fifty-five miles long. Nor is it more satisfactory to suppose that by a city of three days' journey is meant a city which it would require three days to go all over. No intelligible idea of size could possibly be conveyed by such a definition. Adopting, then, the more reasonable view that the "three days' journey" refers to the circumference of the city, and estimating a day's journey at about twenty miles, we have Nineveh here described as comprising a circuit of about sixty miles. Whether this large area was inclosed by continuous walls we cannot certainly say. One ancient writer, indeed, (Diodorus Siculus) asserts that it was, and that the walls were "100 feet high, and broad enough for three chariots to drive abreast upon" (*Dict. of Bible*, Article *Nineveh*); and he, moreover, gives the dimensions of the city as an irregular quadrangle of about 60 miles in circuit. But without relying too much upon his testimony, which may be regarded as doubtful, we may conclude that an area such as has been described was sufficiently marked out to be known and spoken of as the city of Nineveh. This vast area was not, however, completely covered as in the case of our own cities, with streets and squares and buildings. That was a feature unusual, and almost unknown, in the ancient cities of the East. It was perhaps the feature which, belonging to Jerusalem by virtue of the deep ravines by which it was surrounded, and which "determined its natural boundaries," and prevented its spreading abroad after the fashion of other oriental cities, called forth the surprise and admiration of the Jews after their return from Babylon. "Jerusalem," they exclaim, "(unlike Babylon where we so long have dwelt) is built as a city which is compact together." Like Babylon, Nineveh included not only parks and paradises, but fields under tillage and pastures for "much cattle" (iv. 11) in its wide embrace. The most probable site of the city thus defined will be seen by reference to the accompanying plan. It lies on the eastern bank of the Tigris in the fork formed by that river and the Ghazr Su and Great Zab, just above their confluence. The whole of this district abounds in heaps of ruins. Indeed, "they are found," it is said, "in vast numbers throughout the whole region watered by the Tigris and Euphrates and their confluents, from the Taurus to the Persian Gulf." "Such mounds," it is added, "are especially numerous in the region to the east of the Tigris, in which Nineveh stood, and some of them must mark the ruins of the Assyrian capital." (*Dict. of the Bible.*) Four of these great masses of ruins, which will be found marked on the plan, Kouyunjik, Nimrud, Karamless, Khorsabad, form together an irregular parallelogram of very similar dimensions to those mentioned in the text. From Kouyunjik (lying opposite Mosul) on the Eastern bank of the Tigris, a line drawn in a S.E. direction, parallel to the course of the river, to Nimrud is about eighteen miles. From Nimrud, in a northerly direction, to Karamless is about twelve.

The opposite sides of the parallelogram, from Karamless to the most northerly point Khorsabad, and from Khorsabad to Kouyunjik again, are about the same. These four vast piles of buildings, with the area included in the parallelogram which they form, are now generally identified with the site of the Nineveh which Jonah visited. For fuller particulars the reader is referred to Smith's *Dictionary of the Bible*, Article *Nineveh*, and to the well-known works of Mr Layard and Professor Rawlinson.

INDEX.

CAMBRIDGE: PRINTED BY C. J. CLAY, M.A. AND SONS, AT THE UNIVERSITY PRESS.

THE CAMBRIDGE BIBLE FOR SCHOOLS AND COLLEGES.

GENERAL EDITOR, THE VERY REV. J. J. S. PEROWNE,
DEAN OF PETERBOROUGH.

Opinions of the Press.

"*It is difficult to commend too highly this excellent series.*"—Guardian.

"*The modesty of the general title of this series has, we believe, led many to misunderstand its character and underrate its value. The books are well suited for study in the upper forms of our best schools, but not the less are they adapted to the wants of all Bible students who are not specialists. We doubt, indeed, whether any of the numerous popular commentaries recently issued in this country will be found more serviceable for general use.*"—Academy.

"*One of the most popular and useful literary enterprises of the nineteenth century.*"—Baptist Magazine.

"*Of great value. The whole series of comments for schools is highly esteemed by students capable of forming a judgment. The books are scholarly without being pretentious: and information is so given as to be easily understood.*"—Sword and Trowel.

"*The value of the work as an aid to Biblical study, not merely in schools but among people of all classes who are desirous to have intelligent knowledge of the Scriptures, cannot easily be over-estimated.*"—The Scotsman.

The Book of Judges. J. J. LIAS, M.A. "His introduction is clear and concise, full of the information which young students require, and indicating the lines on which the various problems suggested by the Book of Judges may be solved."—*Baptist Magazine.*

1 Samuel, by A. F. KIRKPATRICK. "Remembering the interest with which we read the *Books of the Kingdom* when they were appointed as a subject for school work in our boyhood, we have looked with some eagerness into Mr Kirkpatrick's volume, which contains the first instalment of them. We are struck with the great improvement in character, and variety in the materials, with which schools are now supplied. A clear map inserted in each volume, notes suiting the convenience of the scholar and the difficulty of the passage, and not merely dictated by the fancy of the commentator, were luxuries which a quarter of a century ago the Biblical student could not buy."—*Church Quarterly Review.*

"To the valuable series of Scriptural expositions and elementary commentaries which is being issued at the Cambridge University Press, under the title 'The Cambridge Bible for Schools,' has been added **The First Book of Samuel** by the Rev. A. F. KIRKPATRICK. Like other volumes of the series, it contains a carefully written historical and critical introduction, while the text is profusely illustrated and explained by notes."—*The Scotsman.*

20,000

7/1/90

II. Samuel. A. F. KIRKPATRICK, M.A. "Small as this work is in mere dimensions, it is every way the best on its subject and for its purpose that we know of. The opening sections at once prove the thorough competence of the writer for dealing with questions of criticism in an earnest, faithful and devout spirit; and the appendices discuss a few special difficulties with a full knowledge of the data, and a judicial reserve, which contrast most favourably with the superficial dogmatism which has too often made the exegesis of the Old Testament a field for the play of unlimited paradox and the ostentation of personal infallibility. The notes are always clear and suggestive; never trifling or irrelevant; and they everywhere demonstrate the great difference in value between the work of a commentator who is also a Hebraist, and that of one who has to depend for his Hebrew upon secondhand sources."—*Academy*.

"The Rev. A. F. KIRKPATRICK has now completed his commentary on the two books of Samuel. This second volume, like the first, is furnished with a scholarly and carefully prepared critical and historical introduction, and the notes supply everything necessary to enable the merely English scholar—so far as is possible for one ignorant of the original language—to gather up the precise meaning of the text. Even Hebrew scholars may consult this small volume with profit."—*Scotsman*.

I. Kings and Ephesians. "With great heartiness we commend these most valuable little commentaries. We had rather purchase these than nine out of ten of the big blown up expositions. Quality is far better than quantity, and we have it here."—*Sword and Trowel*.

I. Kings. "This is really admirably well done, and from first to last there is nothing but commendation to give to such honest work."—*Bookseller*.

II. Kings. "The Introduction is scholarly and wholly admirable, while the notes must be of incalculable value to students."—*Glasgow Herald*.

"It is equipped with a valuable introduction and commentary, and makes an admirable text book for Bible-classes."—*Scotsman*.

"It would be difficult to find a commentary better suited for general use."—*Academy*.

The Book of Job. "Able and scholarly as the Introduction is, it is far surpassed by the detailed exegesis of the book. In this Dr DAVIDSON'S strength is at its greatest. His linguistic knowledge, his artistic habit, his scientific insight, and his literary power have full scope when he comes to exegesis. ...The book is worthy of the reputation of Dr Davidson; it represents the results of many years of labour, and it will greatly help to the right understanding of one of the greatest works in the literature of the world."—*The Spectator*.

"In the course of a long introduction, Dr DAVIDSON has presented us with a very able and very interesting criticism of this wonderful book. Its contents, the nature of its composition, its idea and purpose, its integrity, and its age are all exhaustively treated of....We have not space to examine fully the text and notes before us, but we can, and do heartily, recommend the book, not only for the upper forms in schools, but to Bible students and teachers generally. As we wrote of a previous volume in the same series, this one leaves nothing to be desired. The notes are full and suggestive, without being too long, and, in itself, the introduction forms a valuable addition to modern Bible literature."—*The Educational Times.*

"Already we have frequently called attention to this exceedingly valuable work as its volumes have successively appeared. But we have never done so with greater pleasure, very seldom with so great pleasure, as we now refer to the last published volume, that on the **Book of Job**, by Dr DAVIDSON, of Edinburgh....We cordially commend the volume to all our readers. The least instructed will understand and enjoy it; and mature scholars will learn from it."—*Methodist Recorder.*

Job—Hosea. "It is difficult to commend too highly this excellent series, the volumes of which are now becoming numerous. The two books before us, small as they are in size, comprise almost everything that the young student can reasonably expect to find in the way of helps towards such general knowledge of their subjects as may be gained without an attempt to grapple with the Hebrew; and even the learned scholar can hardly read without interest and benefit the very able introductory matter which both these commentators have prefixed to their volumes. It is not too much to say that these works have brought within the reach of the ordinary reader resources which were until lately quite unknown for understanding some of the most difficult and obscure portions of Old Testament literature."—*Guardian.*

Ecclesiastes; or, the Preacher.—"Of the Notes, it is sufficient to say that they are in every respect worthy of Dr PLUMPTRE's high reputation as a scholar and a critic, being at once learned, sensible, and practical.... An appendix, in which it is clearly proved that the author of *Ecclesiastes* anticipated Shakspeare and Tennyson in some of their finest thoughts and reflections, will be read with interest by students both of Hebrew and of English literature. Commentaries are seldom attractive reading. This little volume is a notable exception."—*The Scotsman.*

"In short, this little book is of far greater value than most of the larger and more elaborate commentaries on this Scripture. Indispensable to the scholar, it will render real and large help to all who have to expound the dramatic utterances of **The Preacher** whether in the Church or in the School."—*The Expositor.*

"The '*ideal* biography' of the author is one of the most exquisite and fascinating pieces of writing we have met with, and, granting its starting-point, throws wonderful light on many problems connected with the book. The notes illustrating the text are full of delicate criticism, fine glowing insight, and apt historical allusion. An abler volume than Professor PLUMPTRE's we could not desire."—*Baptist Magazine.*

Jeremiah, by A. W. STREANE. "The arrangement of the book is well treated on pp. xxx., 396, and the question of Baruch's relations with its composition on pp. xxvii., xxxiv., 317. The illustrations from English literature, history, monuments, works on botany, topography, etc., are good and plentiful, as indeed they are in other volumes of this series."—*Church Quarterly Review*, April, 1881.

"Mr STREANE's **Jeremiah** consists of a series of admirable and wellnigh exhaustive notes on the text, with introduction and appendices, drawing the life, times, and character of the prophet, the style, contents, and arrangement of his prophecies, the traditions relating to Jeremiah, meant as a type of Christ (a most remarkable chapter), and other prophecies relating to Jeremiah."—*The English Churchman and Clerical Journal.*

Obadiah and Jonah. "This number of the admirable series of Scriptural expositions issued by the Syndics of the Cambridge University Press is well up to the mark. The numerous notes are excellent. No difficulty is shirked, and much light is thrown on the contents both of Obadiah and Jonah. Scholars and students of to-day are to be congratulated on having so large an amount of information on Biblical subjects, so clearly and ably put together, placed within their reach in such small bulk. To all Biblical students the series will be acceptable, and for the use of Sabbath-school teachers will prove invaluable."—*North British Daily Mail.*

"It is a very useful and sensible exposition of these two Minor Prophets, and deals very thoroughly and honestly with the immense difficulties of the later-named of the two, from the orthodox point of view."—*Expositor.*

"**Haggai and Zechariah.** This interesting little volume is of great value. It is one of the best books in that well-known series of scholarly and popular commentaries, 'the Cambridge Bible for Schools and Colleges' of which Dean Perowne is the General Editor. In the expositions of Archdeacon Perowne we are always sure to notice learning, ability, judgment and reverence .... The notes are terse and pointed, but full and reliable."—*Churchman.*

"**The Gospel according to St Matthew**, by the Rev. A. CARR. The introduction is able, scholarly, and eminently practical, as it bears on the authorship and contents of the Gospel, and the original form in which it is supposed to have been written. It is well illustrated by two excellent maps of the Holy Land and of the Sea of Galilee."—*English Churchman.*

"**St Matthew**, edited by A. CARR, M.A. **The Book of Joshua**, edited by G. F. MACLEAR, D.D. **The General Epistle of St James**, edited by E. H. PLUMPTRE, D.D. The introductions and notes are scholarly, and generally such as young readers need and can appreciate. The maps in both Joshua and Matthew are very good, and all matters of editing are faultless. Professor Plumptre's notes on 'The Epistle of St James' are models of terse, exact, and elegant renderings of the original, which is too often obscured in the authorised version."—*Nonconformist.*

"**St Mark**, with Notes by the Rev. G. F. MACLEAR, D.D. Into this small volume Dr Maclear, besides a clear and able Introduction to the Gospel, and the text of St Mark, has compressed many hundreds of valuable and helpful notes. In short, he has given us a capital manual of the kind required—containing all that is needed to illustrate the text, i.e. all that can be drawn from the history, geography, customs, and manners of the time. But as a handbook, giving in a clear and succinct form the information which a lad requires in order to stand an examination in the Gospel, it is admirable......I can very heartily commend it, not only to the senior boys and girls in our High Schools, but also to Sunday-school teachers, who may get from it the very kind of knowledge they often find it hardest to get."—*Expositor.*

"With the help of a book like this, an intelligent teacher may make 'Divinity' as interesting a lesson as any in the school course. The notes are of a kind that will be, for the most part, intelligible to boys of the lower forms of our public schools; but they may be read with greater profit by the fifth and sixth, in conjunction with the original text."—*The Academy.*

"St Luke. Canon FARRAR has supplied students of the Gospel with an admirable manual in this volume. It has all that copious variety of illustration, ingenuity of suggestion, and general soundness of interpretation which readers are accustomed to expect from the learned and eloquent editor. Any one who has been accustomed to associate the idea of 'dryness' with a commentary, should go to Canon Farrar's St Luke for a more correct impression. He will find that a commentary may be made interesting in the highest degree, and that without losing anything of its solid value. . . . But, so to speak, it is *too good* for some of the readers for whom it is intended."—*The Spectator.*

"Canon FARRAR's contribution to The Cambridge School Bible is one of the most valuable yet made. His annotations on **The Gospel according to St Luke**, while they display a scholarship at least as sound, and an erudition at least as wide and varied as those of the editors of St Matthew and St Mark, are rendered telling and attractive by a more lively imagination, a keener intellectual and spiritual insight, a more incisive and picturesque style. His *St Luke* is worthy to be ranked with Professor Plumptre's *St James*, than which no higher commendation can well be given."—*The Expositor.*

"**St Luke.** Edited by Canon FARRAR, D.D. We have received with pleasure this edition of the Gospel by St Luke, by Canon Farrar. It is another instalment of the best school commentary of the Bible we possess. Of the expository part of the work we cannot speak too highly. It is admirable in every way, and contains just the sort of information needed for Students of the English text unable to make use of the original Greek for themselves."—*The Nonconformist and Independent.*

"As a handbook to the third gospel, this small work is invaluable. The author has compressed into little space a vast mass of scholarly information. . . The notes are pithy, vigorous, and suggestive, abounding in pertinent illustrations from general literature, and aiding the youngest reader to an intelligent appreciation of the text. A finer contribution to 'The Cambridge Bible for Schools' has not yet been made."—*Baptist Magazine.*

"We were quite prepared to find in Canon FARRAR's **St Luke** a masterpiece of Biblical criticism and comment, and we are not disappointed by our examination of the volume before us. It reflects very faithfully the learning and critical insight of the Canon's greatest works, his 'Life of Christ' and his 'Life of St Paul', but differs widely from both in the terseness and condensation of its style. What Canon Farrar has evidently aimed at is to place before students as much information as possible within the limits of the smallest possible space, and in this aim he has hit the mark to perfection."—*The Examiner.*

The Gospel according to St John. "Of the notes we can say with confidence that they are useful, necessary, learned, and brief. To Divinity students, to teachers, and for private use, this compact Commentary will be found a valuable aid to the better understanding of the Sacred Text."—*School Guardian.*

"The new volume of the 'Cambridge Bible for Schools'—the **Gospel according to St John**, by the Rev. A. PLUMMER—shows as careful and thorough work as either of its predecessors. The introduction concisely yet fully describes the life of St John, the authenticity of the Gospel, its characteristics, its relation to the Synoptic Gospels, and to the Apostle's First Epistle, and the usual subjects referred to in an 'introduction'."—*The Christian Church.*

"The notes are extremely scholarly and valuable, and in most cases exhaustive, bringing to the elucidation of the text all that is best in commentaries, ancient and modern."—*The English Churchman and Clerical Journal.*

"(1) **The Acts of the Apostles.** By J. RAWSON LUMBY, D.D. (2) **The Second Epistle of the Corinthians**, edited by Professor LIAS. The introduction is pithy, and contains a mass of carefully-selected information on the authorship of the Acts, its designs, and its sources. ......The Second Epistle of the Corinthians is a manual beyond all praise, for the excellence of its pithy and pointed annotations, its analysis of the contents, and the fulness and value of its introduction."—*Examiner.*

"The concluding portion of the **Acts of the Apostles**, under the very competent editorship of Dr LUMBY, is a valuable addition to our school-books on that subject. Detailed criticism is impossible within the space at our command, but we may say that the ample notes touch with much exactness the very points on which most readers of the text desire information. Due reference is made, where necessary, to the Revised Version; the maps are excellent; and we do not know of any other volume where so much help is given to the complete understanding of one of the most important and, in many respects, difficult books of the New Testament."—*School Guardian.*

"The Rev. H. C. G. MOULE, M.A., has made a valuable addition to THE CAMBRIDGE BIBLE FOR SCHOOLS in his brief commentary on the **Epistle to the Romans.** The 'Notes' are very good, and lean, as the notes of a School Bible should, to the most commonly accepted and orthodox view of the inspired author's meaning; while the Introduction, and especially the Sketch of the Life of St Paul, is a model of condensation. It is as lively and pleasant to read as if two or three facts had not been crowded into well-nigh every sentence."—*Expositor.*

"**The Epistle to the Romans.** It is seldom we have met with a work so remarkable for the compression and condensation of all that is valuable in the smallest possible space as in the volume before us. Within its limited pages we have 'a sketch of the Life of St Paul,' we have further a critical account of the date of the Epistle to the Romans, of its language, and of its genuineness. The notes are numerous, full of matter, to the point, and leave no real difficulty or obscurity unexplained."—*The Examiner.*

"**The First Epistle to the Corinthians.** Edited by Professor LIAS. Every fresh instalment of this annotated edition of the Bible for Schools confirms the favourable opinion we formed of its value from the examination of its first number. The origin and plan of the Epistle are discussed with its character and genuineness."—*The Nonconformist.*

"**The Second Epistle to the Corinthians.** By Professor LIAS. **The General Epistles of St Peter and St Jude.** By E. H. PLUMPTRE, D.D. We welcome these additions to the valuable series of the Cambridge Bible. We have nothing to add to the commendation which we have from the first publication given to this edition of the Bible. It is enough to say that Professor Lias has completed his work on the two Epistles to the Corinthians in the same admirable manner as at first. Dr Plumptre has also completed the Catholic Epistles."—*Nonconformist.*

The Epistle to the Ephesians. By Rev. H. C. G. MOULE, M.A. "It seems to us the model of a School and College Commentary—comprehensive, but not cumbersome; scholarly, but not pedantic."—*Baptist Magazine.*

The Epistle to the Philippians. "There are few series more valued by theological students than 'The Cambridge Bible for Schools and Colleges,' and there will be no number of it more esteemed than that by Mr H. C. G. MOULE on the *Epistle to the Philippians.*"—*Record.*

"Another capital volume of 'The Cambridge Bible for Schools and Colleges.' The notes are a model of scholarly, lucid, and compact criticism."—*Baptist Magazine.*

Hebrews. "Like his (Canon Farrar's) commentary on Luke it possesses all the best characteristics of his writing. It is a work not only of an accomplished scholar, but of a skilled teacher."—*Baptist Magazine.*

"We heartily commend this volume of this excellent work."—*Sunday School Chronicle.*

"**The General Epistle of St James**, by Professor PLUMPTRE, D.D. Nevertheless it is, so far as I know, by far the best exposition of the Epistle of St James in the English language. Not Schoolboys or Students going in for an examination alone, but Ministers and Preachers of the Word, may get more real help from it than from the most costly and elaborate commentaries."—*Expositor.*

The Epistles of St John. By the Rev. A. PLUMMER, M.A., D.D. "This forms an admirable companion to the 'Commentary on the Gospel according to St John,' which was reviewed in *The Churchman* as soon as it appeared. Dr Plummer has some of the highest qualifications for such a task; and these two volumes, their size being considered, will bear comparison with the best Commentaries of the time."—*The Churchman.*

"Dr PLUMMER's edition of **the Epistles of St John** is worthy of its companions in the 'Cambridge Bible for Schools' Series. The subject, though not apparently extensive, is really one not easy to treat, and requiring to be treated at length, owing to the constant reference to obscure heresies in the Johannine writings. Dr Plummer has done his exegetical task well."—*The Saturday Review.*

THE CAMBRIDGE GREEK TESTAMENT

FOR SCHOOLS AND COLLEGES

with a Revised Text, based on the most recent critical authorities, and English Notes, prepared under the direction of the General Editor,

THE VERY REVEREND J. J. S. PEROWNE, D.D.

"*Has achieved an excellence which puts it above criticism.*"—Expositor.

St Matthew. "Copious illustrations, gathered from a great variety of sources, make his notes a very valuable aid to the student. They are indeed remarkably interesting, while all explanations on meanings, applications, and the like are distinguished by their lucidity and good sense."—*Pall Mall Gazette.*

St Mark. "The Cambridge Greek Testament of which Dr MACLEAR'S edition of the Gospel according to St Mark is a volume, certainly supplies a want. Without pretending to compete with the leading commentaries, or to embody very much original research, it forms a most satisfactory introduction to the study of the New Testament in the original....Dr Maclear's introduction contains all that is known of St Mark's life; an account of the circumstances in which the Gospel was composed, with an estimate of the influence of St Peter's teaching upon St Mark; an excellent sketch of the special characteristics of this Gospel; an analysis, and a chapter on the text of the New Testament generally."—*Saturday Review.*

St Luke. "Of this second series we have a new volume by Archdeacon FARRAR on *St Luke*, completing the four Gospels....It gives us in clear and beautiful language the best results of modern scholarship. We have a most attractive *Introduction.* Then follows a sort of composite Greek text, representing fairly and in very beautiful type the consensus of modern textual critics. At the beginning of the exposition of each chapter of the Gospel are a few short critical notes giving the manuscript evidence for such various readings as seem to deserve mention. The expository notes are short, but clear and helpful. For young students and those who are not disposed to buy or to study the much more costly work of Godet, this seems to us to be the best book on the Greek Text of the Third Gospel."—*Methodist Recorder.*

St John. "We take this opportunity of recommending to ministers on probation, the very excellent volume of the same series on this part of the New Testament. We hope that most or all of our young ministers will prefer to study the volume in the *Cambridge Greek Testament for Schools.*"—*Methodist Recorder.*

The Acts of the Apostles. "Professor LUMBY has performed his laborious task well, and supplied us with a commentary the fulness and freshness of which Bible students will not be slow to appreciate. The volume is enriched with the usual copious indexes and four coloured maps."—*Glasgow Herald.*

I. Corinthians. "Mr LIAS is no novice in New Testament exposition, and the present series of essays and notes is an able and helpful addition to the existing books."—*Guardian.*

The Epistles of St John. "In the very useful and well annotated series of the Cambridge Greek Testament the volume on the Epistles of St John must hold a high position...The notes are brief, well informed and intelligent."—*Scotsman.*

CAMBRIDGE: PRINTED BY C. J. CLAY, M.A. AND SONS, AT THE UNIVERSITY PRESS.

CAMBRIDGE UNIVERSITY PRESS.

THE PITT PRESS SERIES.

₊ *Many of the books in this list can be had in two volumes, Text and Notes separately.*

I. GREEK.

Aristophanes. Aves—Plutus—Ranæ. By W. C. GREEN, M.A., late Assistant Master at Rugby School. 3s. 6d. each.

Aristotle. Outlines of the Philosophy of. Compiled by EDWIN WALLACE, M.A., LL.D. Third Edition, Enlarged. 4s. 6d.

Euripides. Heracleidae. With Introduction and Explanatory Notes. By E. A. BECK, M.A., Fellow of Trinity Hall. 3s. 6d.

—— **Hercules Furens.** With Introduction, Notes and Analysis. By A. GRAY, M.A., and J. T. HUTCHINSON, M.A. New Ed. 2s.

—— **Hippolytus.** With Introduction and Notes. By W. S. HADLEY, M.A., Fellow of Pembroke College. 2s.

——— **Iphigeneia in Aulis.** By C. E. S. HEADLAM, B.A. 2s. 6d.

Herodotus, Book V. Edited with Notes and Introduction by E. S. SHUCKBURGH, M.A. 3s.

—— **Book VI.** By the same Editor. 4s.

—— **Book VIII., Chaps. 1—90.** By the same Editor. 3s. 6d.

—— **Book IX., Chaps. 1—89.** By the same Editor. 3s. 6d.

Homer. Odyssey, Books IX., X. With Introduction, Notes and Appendices by G. M. EDWARDS, M.A. 2s. 6d. each.

—— —— **Book XXI.** By the same Editor. 2s.

Luciani Somnium Charon Piscator et De Luctu. By W. E. HEITLAND, M.A., Fellow of St John's College, Cambridge. 3s. 6d.

Platonis Apologia Socratis. With Introduction, Notes and Appendices. By J. ADAM, M.A. 3s. 6d.

—— **Crito.** By the same Editor. 2s. 6d.

—— **Euthyphro.** By the same Editor. [*In the Press.*

Plutarch. Lives of the Gracchi. With Introduction, Notes and Lexicon by Rev. H. A. HOLDEN, M.A., LL.D. 6s.

—— **Life of Nicias.** By the same Editor. 5s.

—— **Life of Sulla.** By the same Editor. 6s.

—— **Life of Timoleon.** By the same Editor. 6s.

Sophocles. Oedipus Tyrannus. School Edition, with Introduction and Commentary by R. C. JEBB, Litt.D., LL.D. 4s. 6d.

Xenophon. Agesilaus. By H. HAILSTONE, M.A. 2s. 6d.

—— **Anabasis.** With Introduction, Map and English Notes, by A. PRETOR, M.A. Two vols. 7s. 6d.

—— **Books I. III. IV. and V.** By the same. 2s. each.

—— **Books II. VI. and VII.** By the same. 2s. 6d. each.

Xenophon. Cyropaedeia. Books I. II. With Introduction and Notes by Rev. H. A. HOLDEN, M.A., LL.D. 2 vols. 6s.

—— —— **Books III. IV. and V.** By the same Editor. 5s.

London: Cambridge Warehouse, Ave Maria Lane.

25/2/'90

II. LATIN.

Beda's Ecclesiastical History, Books III., IV. Edited with a life, Notes, Glossary, Onomasticon and Index, by J. E. B. MAYOR, M.A., and J. R. LUMBY, D.D. Revised Edition. 7s. 6d.
—— **Books I. II.** By the same Editors. [*In the Press.*

Caesar. De Bello Gallico, Comment. I. With Maps and Notes by A. G. PESKETT, M.A., Fellow of Magdalene College, Cambridge. 1s. 6d. COMMENT. II. III. 2s. COMMENT. I. II. III. 3s. COMMENT. IV. V., and COMMENT. VII. 2s. each. COMMENT. VI. and COMMENT. VIII. 1s. 6d. each.

Cicero. De Amicitia.—De Senectute. Edited by J. S. REID, Litt.D., Fellow of Gonville and Caius College. 3s. 6d. each.
—— **In Gaium Verrem Actio Prima.** With Notes, by H. COWIE, M.A. 1s. 6d.
—— **In Q. Caecilium Divinatio et in C. Verrem Actio.** With Notes by W. E. HEITLAND, M.A., and H. COWIE, M.A. 3s.
—— **Philippica Secunda.** By A. G. PESKETT, M.A. 3s. 6d.
—— **Oratio pro Archia Poeta.** By J. S. REID, Litt.D. 2s.
—— **Pro L. Cornelio Balbo Oratio.** By the same. 1s. 6d.
—— **Oratio pro Tito Annio Milone,** with English Notes, &c., by JOHN SMYTH PURTON, B.D. 2s. 6d.
—— **Oratio pro L. Murena,** with English Introduction and Notes. By W. E. HEITLAND, M.A. 3s.
—— **Pro Cn. Plancio Oratio,** by H. A. HOLDEN, LL.D. 4s.6d.
—— **Pro P. Cornelio Sulla.** By J. S. REID, Litt.D. 3s. 6d.
—— **Somnium Scipionis.** With Introduction and Notes. Edited by W. D. PEARMAN, M.A. 2s.

Horace. Epistles, Book I. With Notes and Introduction by E. S. SHUCKBURGH, M.A., late Fellow of Emmanuel College. 2s. 6d.

Livy. Book IV. With Introduction and Notes. By H. M. STEPHENSON, M.A. 2s. 6d.
—— **Book V.** With Introduction and Notes by L. WHIBLEY, M.A. 2s. 6d.
—— **Books XXI., XXII.** With Notes, Introduction and Maps. By M. S. DIMSDALE, M.A., Fellow of King's College. 2s. 6d. each.

Lucan. Pharsaliae Liber Primus, with English Introduction and Notes by W. E. HEITLAND, M.A., and C. E. HASKINS, M.A. 1s. 6d.

Lucretius, Book V. With Notes and Introduction by J. D. DUFF, M.A., Fellow of Trinity College. 2s.

Ovidii Nasonis Fastorum Liber VI. With Notes by A. SIDGWICK, M.A., Tutor of Corpus Christi College, Oxford. 1s. 6d.

Quintus Curtius. A Portion of the History (Alexander in India). By W. E. HEITLAND, M.A., and T. E. RAVEN, B.A. With Two Maps. 3s. 6d.

Vergili Maronis Aeneidos Libri I.—XII. Edited with Notes by A. SIDGWICK, M.A. 1s. 6d. each.
—— **Bucolica.** By the same Editor. 1s. 6d
—— **Georgicon Libri I. II.** By the same Editor. 2s.
—— —— **Libri III. IV.** By the same Editor. 2s.
—— **The Complete Works.** By the same Editor. Two vols. Vol. I. containing the Text. Vol. II. The Notes. [*Preparing.*

III. FRENCH.

Corneille. La Suite du Menteur. A Comedy in Five Acts.
With Notes Philological and Historical, by the late G. MASSON, B.A. 2s.

De Bonnechose. Lazare Hoche. With four Maps, Introduction and Commentary, by C. COLBECK, M.A. Revised Edition. 2s.

D'Harleville. Le Vieux Célibataire. A Comedy, Grammatical and Historical Notes, by G. MASSON, B.A. 2s.

De Lamartine. Jeanne D'Arc. Edited with a Map and
Notes Historical and Philological, and a Vocabulary, by Rev. A. C. CLAPIN,
M.A., St John's College, Cambridge. 2s.

De Vigny. La Canne de Jonc. Edited with Notes by
Rev. H. A. BULL, M.A., late Master at Wellington College. 2s.

Erckmann-Chatrian. La Guerre. With Map, Introduction
and Commentary by Rev. A. C. CLAPIN, M.A. 3s.

La Baronne de Staël-Holstein. Le Directoire. (Considéra-
tions sur la Révolution Française. Troisième et quatrième parties.) Revised
and enlarged. With Notes by G. MASSON, B.A., and G. W. PROTHERO, M.A. 2s.

—— —— **Dix Années d'Exil. Livre II. Chapitres 1—8.**
By the same Editors. New Edition, enlarged. 2s.

Lemercier. Fredegonde et Brunehaut. A Tragedy in Five
Acts. By GUSTAVE MASSON, B.A. 2s.

Molière. Le Bourgeois Gentilhomme, Comédie-Ballet en
Cinq Actes. (1670.) By Rev. A. C. CLAPIN, M.A. Revised Edition. 1s. 6d.

—— **L'École des Femmes.** With Introduction and Notes by
G. SAINTSBURY, M.A. 2s. 6d.

—— **Les Précieuses Ridicules.** With Introduction and
Notes by E. G. W. BRAUNHOLTZ, M.A., Ph.D. 2s.

Piron. La Métromanie. A Comedy, with Notes, by G.
MASSON, B.A. 2s.

Racine. Les Plaideurs. With Introduction and Notes, by
E. G. W. BRAUNHOLTZ, M.A., Ph.D. 2s.

Sainte-Beuve. M. Daru (Causeries du Lundi, Vol. IX.).
By G. MASSON, B.A. 2s.

Saintine. Picciola. With Introduction, Notes and Map. By
Rev. A. C. CLAPIN, M.A. 2s.

Scribe and Legouvé. Bataille de Dames. Edited by Rev.
H. A. BULL, M.A. 2s.

Scribe. Le Verre d'Eau. A Comedy; with Memoir, Grammatical and Historical Notes. Edited by C. COLBECK, M.A. 2s.

Sédaine. Le Philosophe sans le savoir. Edited with Notes
by Rev. H. A. BULL, M.A., late Master at Wellington College. 2s.

Thierry. Lettres sur l'histoire de France (XIII.—XXIV.).
By G. MASSON, B.A., and G. W. PROTHERO, M.A. 2s. 6d.

—— **Récits des Temps Mérovingiens I.—III.** Edited by
GUSTAVE MASSON, B.A. Univ. Gallic., and A. R. ROPES, M.A. With Map. 3s.

Villemain. Lascaris ou Les Grecs du XVe Siècle, Nouvelle
Historique. By G. MASSON, B.A. 2s.

London: Cambridge Warehouse, Ave Maria Lane.

Voltaire. Histoire du Siècle de Louis XIV. Chaps. I.—
XIII. Edited by G. MASSON, B.A., and G. W. PROTHERO, M.A. 2s. 6d.
PART II. CHAPS. XIV.—XXIV. By the same Editors. With Three Maps.
2s. 6d. PART III. CHAPS. XXV. to end. By the same Editors. 2s. 6d.

Xavier de Maistre. La Jeune Sibérienne. Le Lépreux de
la Cité D'Aoste. By G. MASSON, B.A. 1s. 6d.

IV. GERMAN.

Ballads on German History. Arranged and annotated by
WILHELM WAGNER, Ph.D. 2s.

Benedix. Doctor Wespe. Lustspiel in fünf Aufzügen. Edited
with Notes by KARL HERMANN BREUL, M.A. 3s.

Freytag. Der Staat Friedrichs des Grossen. With Notes.
By WILHELM WAGNER, Ph.D. 2s.

German Dactylic Poetry. Arranged and annotated by
WILHELM WAGNER, Ph.D. 3s.

Goethe's Knabenjahre. (1749—1759.) Arranged and annotated by WILHELM WAGNER, Ph.D. 2s.

—— **Hermann und Dorothea.** By WILHELM WAGNER,
Ph.D. Revised edition by J. W. CARTMELL, M.A. 3s. 6d.

Gutzkow. Zopf und Schwert. Lustspiel in fünf Aufzügen.
By H J. WOLSTENHOLME, B.A. (Lond.). 3s. 6d.

Hauff. Das Bild des Kaisers. By KARL HERMANN BREUL,
M.A., Ph.D., University Lecturer in German. 3s.

—— **Das Wirthshaus im Spessart.** By A. SCHLOTTMANN,
Ph.D. 3s. 6d.

—— **Die Karavane.** Edited with Notes by A. SCHLOTT-
MANN, Ph.D. 3s. 6d.

Immermann. Der Oberhof. A Tale of Westphalian Life, by
WILHELM WAGNER, Ph.D. 3s.

Kohlrausch. Das Jahr 1813. With English Notes by WILHELM
WAGNER, Ph.D. 2s.

Lessing and Gellert. Selected Fables. Edited with Notes
by KARL HERMANN BREUL, M.A. 3s.

Mendelssohn's Letters. Selections from. Edited by JAMES
SIME, M.A. 3s.

Raumer. Der erste Kreuzzug (1095—1099). By WILHELM
WAGNER, Ph.D. 2s.

Riehl. Culturgeschichtliche Novellen. Edited by H. J.
WOLSTENHOLME, B.A. (Lond.). 3s. 6d.

Schiller. Wilhelm Tell. Edited with Introduction and Notes
by KARL HERMANN BREUL, M.A. 2s. 6d.

Uhland. Ernst, Herzog von Schwaben. With Introduction
and Notes. By H. J. WOLSTENHOLME, B.A. 3s. 6d.

V. ENGLISH.

Ancient Philosophy from Thales to Cicero, A Sketch of. By JOSEPH B. MAYOR, M.A. 3*s.* 6*d.*

Bacon's History of the Reign of King Henry VII. With Notes by the Rev. Professor LUMBY, D.D. 3*s.*

Cowley's Essays. With Introduction and Notes, by the Rev. Professor LUMBY, D.D. 4*s.*

More's History of King Richard III. Edited with Notes, Glossary, Index of Names. By J. RAWSON LUMBY, D.D. 3*s.* 6*d.*

More's Utopia. With Notes, by Rev. Prof. LUMBY, D.D. 3*s.* 6*d.*

The Two Noble Kinsmen, edited with Introduction and Notes, by the Rev. Professor SKEAT, Litt.D. 3*s.* 6*d.*

VI. EDUCATIONAL SCIENCE.

Comenius, John Amos, Bishop of the Moravians. His Life and Educational Works, by S. S. LAURIE, A.M., F.R.S.E. 3*s.* 6*d.*

Education, Three Lectures on the Practice of. I. On Marking, by H. W. EVE, M.A. II. On Stimulus, by A. SIDGWICK, M.A. III. On the Teaching of Latin Verse Composition, by E. A. ABBOTT, D.D. 2*s.*

Stimulus. A Lecture delivered for the Teachers' Training Syndicate, May, 1882, by A. SIDGWICK, M.A. 1*s.*

Locke on Education. With Introduction and Notes by the Rev. R. H. QUICK, M.A. 3*s.* 6*d.*

Milton's Tractate on Education. A facsimile reprint from the Edition of 1673. Edited with Notes, by O. BROWNING, M.A. 2*s.*

Modern Languages, Lectures on the Teaching of. By C. COLBECK, M.A. 2*s.*

Teacher, General Aims of the, and Form Management. Two Lectures delivered in the University of Cambridge in the Lent Term, 1883, by F. W. FARRAR, D.D., and R. B. POOLE, B.D. 1*s.* 6*d.*

Teaching, Theory and Practice of. By the Rev. E. THRING, M.A., late Head Master of Uppingham School. New Edition. 4*s.* 6*d.*

British India, a Short History of. By E. S. CARLOS, M.A., late Head Master of Exeter Grammar School. 1*s.*

Geography, Elementary Commercial. A Sketch of the Commodities and the Countries of the World. By H. R. MILL, D.Sc., F.R.S.E. 1*s.*

Geography, an Atlas of Commercial. (A Companion to the above.) By J. G. BARTHOLOMEW, F.R.G.S. With an Introduction by HUGH ROBERT MILL, D.Sc. 3*s.*

VII. MATHEMATICS.

Euclid's Elements of Geometry. Books I. and II. By H. M. TAYLOR, M.A., Fellow and late Tutor of Trinity College, Cambridge. 1*s.* 6*d.*

Other Volumes are in preparation.

London: Cambridge Warehouse, Ave Maria Lane.

𝕿𝖍𝖊 𝕮𝖆𝖒𝖇𝖗𝖎𝖉𝖌𝖊 𝕭𝖎𝖇𝖑𝖊 𝖋𝖔𝖗 𝕾𝖈𝖍𝖔𝖔𝖑𝖘 𝖆𝖓𝖉 𝕮𝖔𝖑𝖑𝖊𝖌𝖊𝖘.

GENERAL EDITOR: J. J. S. PEROWNE, D.D.,
DEAN OF PETERBOROUGH.

"*It is difficult to commend too highly this excellent series.*—Guardian.

"*The modesty of the general title of this series has, we believe, led many to misunderstand its character and underrate its value. The books are well suited for study in the upper forms of our best schools, but not the less are they adapted to the wants of all Bible students who are not specialists. We doubt, indeed, whether any of the numerous popular commentaries recently issued in this country will be found more serviceable for general use.*"—Academy.

Now Ready. Cloth, Extra Fcap. 8vo. With Maps.

Book of Joshua. By Rev. G. F. MACLEAR, D.D.   2s. 6d.
Book of Judges. By Rev. J. J. LIAS, M.A..   3s. 6d.
First Book of Samuel. By Rev. Prof. KIRKPATRICK, B.D.   3s. 6d.
Second Book of Samuel. By Rev. Prof. KIRKPATRICK, B.D.   3s. 6d.
First Book of Kings. By Rev. Prof. LUMBY, D.D.   3s. 6d.
Second Book of Kings. By Rev. Prof. LUMBY, D.D.   3s. 6d.
Book of Job. By Rev. A. B. DAVIDSON, D.D.   5s.
Book of Ecclesiastes. By Very Rev. E. H. PLUMPTRE, D.D.   5s.
Book of Jeremiah. By Rev. A. W. STREANE, M.A.   4s. 6d.
Book of Hosea. By Rev. T. K. CHEYNE, M.A., D.D.   3s.
Books of Obadiah & Jonah. By Archdeacon PEROWNE.   2s. 6d.
Book of Micah. By Rev. T. K. CHEYNE, M.A., D.D.   1s. 6d.
Books of Haggai & Zechariah. By Archdeacon PEROWNE.   3s.
Gospel according to St Matthew. By Rev. A. CARR, M.A.   2s. 6d.
Gospel according to St Mark. By Rev. G. F. MACLEAR, D.D.   2s. 6d.
Gospel according to St Luke. By Arch. FARRAR, D.D.   4s. 6d.
Gospel according to St John. By Rev. A. PLUMMER, D.D.   4s. 6d.
Acts of the Apostles. By Rev. Prof. LUMBY, D.D.   4s. 6d.
Epistle to the Romans. By Rev. H. C. G. MOULE, M.A.   3s. 6d.
First Corinthians. By Rev. J. J. LIAS, M.A.   With Map.   2s.
Second Corinthians. By Rev. J. J. LIAS, M.A.   With Map.   2s.

London: Cambridge Warehouse, Ave Maria Lane.

Epistle to the Ephesians. By Rev. H. C. G. MOULE, M.A. 2s. 6d.

Epistle to the Philippians. By Rev. H. C. G. MOULE, M.A. 2s. 6d.

Epistle to the Hebrews. By Arch. FARRAR, D.D. 3s. 6d.

General Epistle of St James. By Very Rev. E. H. PLUMPTRE, D.D. 1s. 6d.

Epistles of St Peter and St Jude. By Very Rev. E. H. PLUMPTRE, D.D. 2s. 6d.

Epistles of St John. By Rev. A. PLUMMER, M.A., D.D. 3s. 6d.

Preparing.

Book of Genesis. By Very Rev. the Dean of Peterborough.

Books of Exodus, Numbers and Deuteronomy. By Rev. C. D. GINSBURG, LL.D.

Books of Ezra and Nehemiah. By Rev. Prof. RYLE, M.A.

Book of Psalms. By Rev. Prof. KIRKPATRICK, B.D.

Book of Isaiah. By Prof. W. ROBERTSON SMITH, M.A.

Book of Ezekiel. By Rev. A. B. DAVIDSON, D.D.

Book of Malachi. By Archdeacon PEROWNE.

Epistle to the Galatians. By Rev. E. H. PEROWNE, D.D.

Epistles to the Colossians and Philemon. By Rev. H. C. G. MOULE, M.A.

Epistles to Timothy & Titus. By Rev. A. E. HUMPHREYS, M.A.

Book of Revelation. By Rev. W. H. SIMCOX, M.A.

The Smaller Cambridge Bible for Schools.

The Smaller Cambridge Bible for Schools *will form an entirely new series of commentaries on some selected books of the Bible. It is expected that they will be prepared for the most part by the Editors of the larger series (The Cambridge Bible for Schools and Colleges). The volumes will be issued at a low price, and will be suitable to the requirements of preparatory and elementary schools.*

Now ready.

First and Second Books of Samuel. By Rev. Prof. KIRKPATRICK, B.D. 1s. each.

Gospel according to St Matthew. By Rev. A. CARR, M.A. 1s.

Gospel according to St Mark. By Rev. G. F. MACLEAR, D.D. 1s.

Nearly ready.

Gospel according to St Luke. By Archdeacon FARRAR.

London: Cambridge Warehouse, Ave Maria Lane.

The Cambridge Greek Testament for Schools and Colleges,

with a Revised Text, based on the most recent critical authorities, and English Notes, prepared under the direction of the General Editor,

The Very Reverend J. J. S. PEROWNE, D.D.,
DEAN OF PETERBOROUGH.

Gospel according to St Matthew. By Rev. A. CARR, M.A.
With 4 Maps. 4s. 6d.

Gospel according to St Mark. By Rev. G. F. MACLEAR, D.D.
With 3 Maps. 4s. 6d.

Gospel according to St Luke. By Archdeacon FARRAR.
With 4 Maps. 6s.

Gospel according to St John. By Rev. A. PLUMMER, D.D.
With 4 Maps. 6s.

Acts of the Apostles. By Rev. Professor LUMBY, D.D.
With 4 Maps. 6s.

First Epistle to the Corinthians. By Rev. J. J. LIAS, M.A. 3s.

Second Epistle to the Corinthians. By Rev. J. J. LIAS, M.A.
[*In the Press.*

Epistle to the Hebrews. By Archdeacon FARRAR, D.D. 3s. 6d.

Epistle of St James. By Very Rev. E. H. PLUMPTRE, D.D.
[*Preparing.*

Epistles of St John. By Rev. A. PLUMMER, M.A., D.D. 4s.

London: C. J. CLAY AND SONS,
CAMBRIDGE WAREHOUSE, AVE MARIA LANE.
Glasgow: 263, ARGYLE STREET.
Cambridge: DEIGHTON, BELL AND CO.
Leipzig: F. A. BROCKHAUS.

CAMBRIDGE: PRINTED BY C. J. CLAY, M.A. AND SONS, AT THE UNIVERSITY PRESS.